What is Love?

Anne Kinsey

O mistress mine, where are you roaming?
O, stay and hear your true-love's coming,
That can sing both high and low.
Trip no further, pretty sweeting;
Journeys end in lovers meeting,
Every wise man's son doth know.

What is love? 'Tis not hereafter;
Present mirth hath present laughter;
What's to come is still unsure.
In delay there lies no plenty;
Then come kiss me, sweet-and-twenty;
Youth's a stuff will not endure.

– William Shakespeare
Twelfth Night

England, 1748

Robert Guildford and his riding party made a splendid picture as they rode through the low hills of West Sussex. As they came around a bend, Guildford caught sight of a girl walking along the road. Even from this distance, he could see that she had a luscious shape: her derriere was sweetly rounded, as soft and inviting as a piece of perfectly ripe fruit.

"Robert?" said Sir Ruthven, one of his companions. "Why are you slowing down?"

He didn't answer.

Another said, "So that's what distracted you, Robert. Shall we offer her a ride?"

"No," Guildford said. "Leave her alone."

The girl, hearing the approach of horses, turned. She wore a simple muslin dress buttoned down the front with a soft white scarf draped over her shoulders. She had a gently curving waist that made Guildford want to run his hands over her hips. She quickly turned back around, but not before Guildford caught sight of a face that seemed to be all ovals and milky white skin.

Sir Ruthven trotted right up alongside her. "Are you going far, miss? Perhaps you would like a ride?"

Guildford stopped a few paces ahead and turned around. Seeing the girl's evident fright, he said, "Leave her alone."

Ignoring Guildford, Ruthven said, "A girl has to be careful out here all alone. Allow me to escort you."

"No, really, sir, I'd rather not." Her voice was as sweet as her face.

One of Guildford's companions said, "She has plenty of sense, that's plain. No girl in her right mind would trust herself to you, Ruthven."

The men around Guildford laughed.

"Come on, pretty one," Ruthven insisted, "I'll help you up. Your fine shoes will be ruined by the time you get wherever you're going."

Again all the riders laughed–except Guildford.

"I'll be all right, sir, thank you." Her voice was quieter, and she was evidently trying to hide her fright. She kept her face averted, but Guildford could see the blush that spread over her neck. Her embarrassment brought out his protective instincts.

"Leave her alone," Guildford said, this time in the tone he reserved for commands. "She said no and she evidently knows her own mind. Come on."

"Robert–"

"I said, leave her alone." To the girl he said, "Forgive our intrusion, Miss."

She looked up at him with such awe and gratitude that he melted completely. She was even more beautiful than he had thought at first. In her face, sweetness and sensuality were perfectly blended.

Her eyes were such a deep blue they were almost purple, reminding him of the blue star sapphire in the brooch his mother used to wear. The light seemed to gather around her.

She carried a small knapsack. For a moment he thought maybe Ruthven was right: A girl like her should not be traveling alone. At least if he and his companions offered her a ride, Guildford could take care to see that no harm came to her.

But Guildford had no desire to see his companions make sport of her. He touched the brim of his hat in a gesture like a salute, then spurred his horse and galloped away, knowing his companions would follow.

He felt restless now, spurring his horse faster, gripping the reins as if motion would ease his turbulence. He hated to gallop away and leave her behind, but he did have four companions with him, so there was little else he could do. Had he been alone, he would certainly have stopped and at least cajoled her into telling him her name and where she lived. He had the feeling if he could be alone with her, he could win her trust and perhaps even tempt her into his arms.

"Ho, Robert," said Carlyle, one of his companions. "Why did you make us leave? Did you see that face?"

"She wants to be left alone," Guildford said.

"She *wants*-?" said one of his companions. Guildford spurred his horse and galloped ahead.

For several minutes the only sound was the clapping of hooves against the road and the faint jingling of harness bells. He felt completely chivalrous.

Ruthven said, "I think I know why Robert made us leave. I'll wager he already knows her. We are not far from his manor house. Guildford, tell the truth, is she on your list of planned conquests?"

"I've never seen her before in my life."

"He is behaving oddly," Ruthven said. "Do you know what I think? I think he has fallen in love with that girl!"

This bit of nonsense brought Guildford out of his reverie. "I have not fallen in love, my friends, nor do I expect to."

"Now he's talking like himself again," said Carlyle.

Julia Brandon watched the riders gallop away, weak with relief. If the gentleman wearing the striped waistcoat hadn't intervened, who knows what they would have done. She imagined he was a great lord who still held to the old code of chivalry.

It wasn't his air of authority, though, which had so captivated her. There was a sparkle in his eye, and something like laughter in his face, as if nothing bad dared happen in his presence. He looked at her with a gentleness that seemed utterly at odds with his grand appearance and powerful body, the way she had always imagined her husband would look at her some day, with a kind of intensity and desire mixed with love and sweetness and compassion. Astonished by her own reaction, she thought it a pity that she should feel so stirred by a stranger on the road who she would probably never see again.

Her father had been right, of course when he'd said walking all this way alone was foolish, but there was no money to hire a coach, and besides, how absurd for her to arrive at her new post in a coach, as if she were a great lady. Her father hadn't been able to escort her because of his injured back. Her brother Geoffrey hadn't been able to escort because he was in Newgate Prison in London, which was the source of all the family's troubles.

If her brother hadn't met a nobleman in a duel and wound up in prison, her father wouldn't have lost his position as mayor of Worthing, and she would not be walking alone on the road this morning. How secure and safe her life had seemed just a few short months earlier! Who would have expected her brother's passionate and headstrong nature to bring about her family's ruin?

By the time she reached the front gates of Guildford Manor, her legs ached and a thin film of dust had gathered over her walking boots. She stopped at the gates and wiped her face and hands clean with a kerchief. She wished she could wash her boots before approaching the house, but the best she could do was to wipe them on her kerchief and brush her skirts clean.

The imposing brick facade, with octagonal bay windows, steep roofs, and tall brick chimney stacks rose above her as grandly as a king's palace. She went around back to the servants' entrance. Pausing again to compose herself, she smoothed her skirt and removed her hat. Then, summoning her courage, she reached up and rang the bell.

A slender gray-haired woman answered the door.

"Well, come in," she said. "You must be the new maid. We're expecting you."

Julia stepped inside and found herself in a narrow wood-paneled entryway. She removed her bonnet. "I'm Julia," she said.

"I'm pleased to meet you, Julia. I'm Mrs. Creston. I've been the housekeeper here since before the young Lord Guildford was born. I'll warn you. The house is all in tumults."

Julia couldn't imagine this house, which seemed so staid and calm, in tumults.

An under butler came up behind the gray-haired woman and said, "I'm pleased to meet you, Miss–"

"Julia," she said.

"Julia," he said. "My name is Sam."

"Quit gaping, Sam," Mrs. Creston snapped, "and go about your work." To Julia, she said, "This way."

She led Julia through the parlor into a large gallery where the floor was made of highly polished black and white marble. The gallery was two stories high, with a curving balustrade staircase on either side of the room and two great landings overlooking the room. Into the walls were cut evenly spaced ovals carved with laurel wreaths. In each oval sat a marble bust. The room smelled of lemon polish and rose petals.

Over the mantle hung a full length portrait of a young man wearing a silver-trimmed riding habit of deep woodland green. The young man stood relaxed, holding a leather riding whip while two puppies played at his feet. Most striking was the man's smile, a pure, joyful, radiant smile which lit his handsome features.

A closer look at those features brought Julia up

short. Could it be? Yes, the painting was of the splendid man she had seen earlier, on the road.

"Who is that?" she asked.

"Lord Guildford, of course," said the gray-haired woman.

Lord Guildford? The owner of this house?

"Come this way," said Mrs. Creston. She led Julia up the staircase on the right. Julia followed, turning back to look one last time at the portrait. Her knees felt suddenly weak.

Down a long corridor was another staircase, this one much narrower. Julia guessed they were entering the servant's quarters. Mrs. Creston turned and said, "Before I take you to Lady Cecilia, Lord Guildford's butler wants a word with you. If you want to keep your post, you'll mind what he tells you."

"Yes, ma'am," Julia said. She wanted to know why the house was in tumults, but she didn't dare ask.

At the end of the corridor was a small office with the door opened wide enough for Julia to see inside. There was a small, cozy fireplace in the corner with a mantle containing a single vase with fresh flowers. Inside at a desk sat a man wearing a black coat. When Mrs. Creston knocked, the man stood up and said, "Enter."

Mrs. Creston entered the office with Julia following. "I've brought Lady Cecilia's new maid. Julia, this is Mr. Ames, Lord Guildford's butler."

Julia bobbed a quick curtsey.

Mr. Ames peered at her. "This one looks like she'll be trouble," he said. "Who hired her?"

"Lady Cecilia, sir. Lord Guildford gave her permission to select her next maid."

"I am surprised. After the trouble Lady Cecilia has been in lately, I am astonished her brother trusts her to make such a choice." To Julia he said, "I am giving you strict orders directly from Lord Guildford himself. His sister Lady Cecilia is not to receive or send letters without his permission."

"Yes, sir," Julia said. When she swallowed she discovered how dry her throat was. She felt she should curtsey again, but her knees felt too stiff to manage it.

"I have no doubt," said Mr. Ames, "that Lady Cecilia will try to persuade you to smuggle letters for her. Take care that you do not become embroiled in her schemes unless you want to be sent from the house in disgrace."

"I understand, sir." Julia hoped she sounded calm and confident.

Mr. Ames handed her a sealed envelope. "Here are your wages for the next three months. This envelope contains six pounds. You may take the money now, or I can keep it here, in the locked safe."

"I would like to have my wages sent to my parents, sir, if you please."

He blinked in evident surprise. "The entire sum?"

"Yes, sir, the entire sum."

A moment passed. He handed her the envelope. "If you write the direction to your parents," he said, his voice softer, "I will see that your wages are sent to them."

"Thank you, sir," Julia said, taking the pen he offered. She paused for a moment. If she wrote "Mr. and Mrs. John Brandon," someone in this house might recognize the name from the recent scandals. To be safe, she wrote "John and Alice" and their new street address in the town of Burgess Hill.

She handed the envelope back to Mr. Ames. He tapped the envelope thoughtfully against the side of the desk. "That is all. You may present her to the earl. Then you may take her to Lady Cecilia."

Julia followed Mrs. Creston back into the corridor.

Mrs. Creston turned and said, "I trust you know the proper way to conduct yourself in the earl's presence."

"I do, ma'am."

"Good. As you will see when you meet him, the earl is not well. He has a sickness which causes him to tremble and makes walking difficult. He speaks very little. Lord Guildford, his nephew and heir, has assumed the responsibilities for the earldom."

Mrs. Creston turned and marched back down the narrow corridor, up a narrow set of stairs, and then into a large gallery with railings overlooking a large gallery on the floor below. To the left was a narrow door.

Mrs. Creston knocked and waited. She heard nothing, so she opened the door a crack and said, "Your lordship? May I bring in the new lady's maid?"

Julia heard no response, but the earl must have nodded or given some signal, because Mrs. Creston, entered the room, gesturing for Julia to follow. There, in a wingback chair near a window, was an elderly man, finely dressed in a white ruffled shirt. He was so thin and fragile Julia wondered if he was able to stand at all on his own legs. There was indeed a slight tremor in his limbs, like reeds quivering in a breeze.

Mrs. Creston stood back so Julia could enter. Julia

stepped forward and curtseyed deeply.

The earl looked at her without blinking. "Step closer," he said.

She took two steps closer, enough to obey his command but not so much as to seem impertinent. He looked at her for so long, she suspected he'd gone into a trance.

"Who—?" he said the word in a raspy voice, then stopped. He breathed deeply and a tremor went through him. Then, in the same throaty whisper, he said, "Who are your people?"

She swallowed. It was the question nobody had asked her. She searched for a truthful but unrevealing answer. "My parents are kind people—"

He closed his eyes and leaned back against the chair. Alarmed, she looked at Mrs. Creston who took her by the arm, and steered her toward the door.

Once they were in the corridor, Mrs. Creston whispered, "There are those who say the old earl has lost his wits, but I don't believe it. Always take great care around him. He may have abdicated his authority, but he is still the earl."

As if Julia needed such a warning!

"This way," Mrs. Creston said. At the top of the stairs and to the left, Mrs. Creston stopped and opened a door.

Inside was a narrow room with a small fireplace and a curtained window overlooking the garden. The room contained two neatly made beds and a wardrobe. The walls were painted the palest shade of ice blue, the curtains white and lacy. It was a simple, demure room, tasteful without being overdone. The rest of the house was large in scale, but this room reminded her of her old bedroom in Worthing.

Instantly she felt comfortable.

"You can put your parcel in here," Mrs. Creston said. "You'll share this room with Blanche, Lady Cecilia's other lady's maid. These are for you." Mrs. Creston handed her a white linen apron and matching mob cap. Julia put the mob cap on, tucking her hair underneath. She caught a glimpse of herself in the small square mirror mounted on the inside door of the wardrobe. The white frills of the mob cap gently framed her face. How strange it felt put on an apron and mob cap and at the same time put on a new identity.

"This door leads to Lady Cecilia's apartments," Mrs. Creston explained, "but we will enter through the main door."

Julia had expected to be assigned a bedroom in the servant's quarters. "Is it customary here for the lady's maids to share the ladies' own chambers?"

"Ever since the troubles began, this is what Lady Cecilia wants. Because of the restrictions on her, she doesn't see her friends any more, so her lady's maids are her only companions."

"I see," said Julia.

Mrs. Creston led Julia back outside into the main corridor, and then she tapped on the next door. This doorway was wider and framed with marble columns.

Lady Cecilia called from inside, "Enter."

Mrs. Creston opened the door and gestured for Julia to go in.

Inside, Lady Cecilia was seated in front of a mirror while another lady's maid, who Julia assumed must be Blanche, combed Lady Cecilia's hair. Blanche was wearing a stripped cotton gown and a

13

mob cap and white apron just like the ones Julia wore. Lady Cecilia was about Julia's age, but she thought Blanche seemed older, perhaps twenty-seven or twenty-eight.

Unlike the small side room Julia would share with Blanche, this room was large and spacious and done in pale pink and lavender, which Julia found a touch too sweet for her taste.

Lady Cecilia glanced at Julia in the mirror. Julia bobbed a curtsey, thinking that anyone watching her would suppose she'd been raised to be a lady's maid.

"How pretty you are!" Lady Cecilia said, turning around. "I'd quite forgotten. Isn't she lovely, Blanche?"

Blanche said, "Indeed she is, my lady."

Julia was thinking that Lady Cecilia was pretty, too, prettier than she remembered.

"I should have warned you when I offered you this position," Lady Cecilia said, "that you are entering a dreary prison."

"Prison, my lady?"

"My brother all but keeps me locked in a prison."

It didn't seem possible to Julia that the gentleman she had met on the road could behave so harshly and unkindly.

"I have nothing for you to do now, Julia, so you may sit here and talk to us while Blanche combs out my hair."

Julia sat on a silver-fringed stool.

"I understand," Blanche said, "you come from Burgess Hill."

"My family has been living there for some time," Julia said evasively.

"I have cousins in Burgess Hill," said Blanche.

Julia shifted uncomfortably. "Who are your cousins?"

"My cousin is Jake the wheelwright."

Fortunately Julia knew who he was. "Ah, yes," she said, "a delightful old man. He and his wife are charming."

"So, Julia," said Lady Cecilia, "has anyone given you orders not to send letters for me?"

"Mr. Ames did, yes."

"Ah. Now Mr. Ames is to lord over me as well. He is even worse than my brother. His new power has gone straight to his head."

"Ah, madam," said Blanche, "I'm sure all these troubles will be over soon and you'll be reconciled to your brother."

"Never! Not as long as he keeps me imprisoned here. I know why you don't want to hear anything said against my brother. You have fallen in love with him, as has every other girl who enters this house, although for the life of me I do not know why! Never mind. I do know why. My brother is too handsome for his own good and can charm anyone into believing anything about him."

"How could a simple girl like me presume to love a great lord like your brother?" said Blanche.

"I know what I know," said Lady Cecilia. To Julia she said, "I hope you won't fall in love with my brother as well, Julia. Perhaps you can keep your wits about yourself and counsel Blanche as to how hopeless her love for him is."

"I would never look so far above myself," Blanche said.

"We'll see. He's as much a tyrant over foolish maids as he is over helpless sisters." Lady Cecilia

15

looked at Julia and laughed. "Tell me what you are thinking. You look positively bewildered."

"I must say, my lady, your description of your brother is bewildering, and alarming as well."

"My brother is charming, and wily, and smart, and I've never yet met a girl able to resist him."

Julia and Blanche ate their midday meal in the servant's dining room at a large oaken trestle table, presided over by the butler at one end and the housekeeper at the other. Julia ate in silence, feeling the curious gaze of the others on her. Sam, the under butler who she had met earlier, tried to engage her in conversation, but she evaded him.

After their meal, she and Blanche returned to find Lady Cecilia sitting at her mirror, tears streaming down her face.

"What happened!" Blanche cried.

"Sir Ruthven is here! In this house! My brother and uncles have ordered me to go downstairs to hear his proposals."

"Oh, my lady," Blanche said comfortingly, sitting beside her on the bed.

"They will not let up on me until I give in! They think they have to guard me, or watch me. I don't know what they think I'm planning to do. How can I run away? I have no place to go. I can't marry the man I have chosen, my uncles have seen to that."

Blanche touched Cecilia's shoulder and said, "I'm sure your uncles will try to find a compromise–"

"I'm afraid, Blanche, they will never compromise.

They are determined that I shall marry Sir Ruthven. How can they even think of such a man for me? Even if I didn't love another, I would never have Sir Ruthven! And now I have to go downstairs to meet him!"

Soon a soft knock came at the door. Blanche opened the door. One of Cecilia's aunts had come for her.

After they left, Blanche took out a sewing basket and a stack of Cecilia's clothes which needed mending. Blanche and Julia sat together, sewing, until at last all the lace was properly fastened, missing buttons had been replaced, and falling hems had been secured. When they finished, Julia sat in the window seat looking into the garden. What she wished, just then, was for the luxury of being entirely alone.

"Do you think," she asked timidly, "I might go for a walk in the garden?"

"I don't see why not. I'll wait here in case she comes back. But stay back from the house."

So Julia left the room and found the back stairs, then a back door leading to the garden. Once outside, she walked past the trimmed box shrubs, keeping out of view of the windows.

Across a lawn, she saw a garden house. What a relief it would be to close a door behind her and escape from the strain of adjusting to a new place and a new position. Up close she found that it wasn't a house at all, but a simple gazebo with a trellised roof, a paved floor, and benches set inside in a half circle.

Once inside and completely hidden, she sank into a bench closed her eyes.

She turned when she heard footsteps.

"It's you!" came a male voice.

Julia leapt to her feet, startled out of her senses. Standing there, larger than life, was Lord Guildford. He smiled so broadly she thought he would laugh. Instinctively she took a step back. The only word she could think of to describe him was beautiful, a word which seemed completely wrong for a man who exuded such strength and masculinity. But he was beautiful with finely chiseled jaw and hair as glossy as a newly brushed colt.

"Tell me who you are," he said gently.

"My name is Julia Dale. I am your sister's new lady's maid."

"But—" he seemed genuinely bewildered. He looked her over from head to toe. "To think you should have a position here, in my house. What good fortune."

She felt entirely flustered. His smile seemed easy and natural.

"I have a confession to make, Julia. The moment I saw you on the road, I knew one day I would make you mine."

She should have felt panic. Instead, she felt herself flushing with pleasure. He looked at her such tenderness, and spoke with such sincerity. Can it be? She wondered. Can people really fall in love this fast?

"Come out tomorrow morning," he said, "at sunrise. I will send word that I have given you the day off—"

"Come out?" Both her hands flew to her mouth when she realized she'd interrupted him. Then she cried, "I cannot take off my second day!"

"Is this not my house? Do I not make the rules? Come to the stables. I will have two horses ready and we can go riding."

She had a vision of herself galloping beside him, her hair blowing behind her in the wind. Her heart quickened at the thought.

"Have you ever gone riding through these hills?" he asked. "They are lovely beyond compare, Julia. I will be waiting. Please don't disappoint me."

Then, very easily, in a fluid motion, he stepped forward and slipped his arm behind her back and drew her to him. "You are so incredibly beautiful," he whispered, and then lowered his lips to hers. For a moment she held perfectly still, feeling his hands tighten behind her back. His lips on hers were gentle, undemanding. Startled, she relaxed into him, content just for the moment to feel the warmth of his body pressing close to her.

She snapped back to the reality of the moment and twisted her face away. She almost said, how dare you! Then she remembered he was the owner of the house, and she a mere lady's maid. She knew very well how he dared.

"Julia," he whispered his tone pleading. She wriggled her hands until they were against his chest. She pushed against him as hard as she could. Still he didn't budge, until with real terror, she said, "Please!"

He loosened his hold on her. "I'm sorry, Julia, I moved too quickly. Please forgive me."

"No," she said, "we can't let this happen." She pulled herself up straight. "Nothing must pass between us that is not proper between a master and servant."

"Oh, Julia!" Then, softening, he said, "I will prove to you that I am worthy of your love."

My brother is as much a tyrant over foolish maids as he is over helpless sisters, Lady Cecilia had said.

"I will wait for you at the stables tomorrow morning," he said, "an hour before daybreak. And I will think about you each minute until then."

She turned and fled from the gazebo into the bright sunlight.

Once inside the house, she climbed the stairs slowly to calm herself. On the landing, she paused, pretending to admire the paintings that hung there. Then, distracted by the paintings, she *did* stop to admire them. At the top of the stairs was a painting of what appeared to be a Biblical scene of Moses. The exquisite play of light on the faces made Julia think she was looking at a genuine Rembrandt. She stood gazing at the painting, feeling that she had been transported to a magical world.

She didn't hear the approaching footsteps until she sensed someone standing very near her.

She whirled around and found herself face to face with the old earl himself. He was leaning against a special cane with a broad, sturdy base.

Recovering her surprise, she curtseyed deeply. "My lord!" she said.

He smiled, but said nothing. Alarmed, she looked around. They were entirely alone. He waited as if expecting her to speak.

"My lord, I was on my way back to Lady Cecilia's

rooms when saw this painting! It's so lovely!" she turned back to the picture. "I think its Moses. Just looking at it, I can feel his pain, his longing, the burden he carries."

She looked back at the old earl, who was still smiling.

How unnerving this was! "I'd almost think it's a real Rembrandt," she said.

"It is a real Rembrandt." His voice was a hoarse whisper. "Now if you will pull that bell for me —" he gestured to a bell in a corner. She pulled the cord and in under a minute a footman came hurrying down the corridor.

"My lord," he said, "let me help you back to your rooms."

Julia had not expected to feel so awkward and self-conscious in her new position. She felt entirely out of place. Oh, what on earth was she doing here!

Her mother's plan for getting the family out of their financial difficulties had been to find a wealthy husband for Julia. Her idea had been to borrow the money to send Julia to London for a season so she could catch a rich husband. One problem with the scheme was if Julia failed to find a suitable husband, her parents would be further in debt. Julia thought there was a good chance their plan would fail. Those in London had a way of finding out a newcomer's family background, and Julia would be subjected to humiliating whispers and jeers.

But Julia's mother was confident that she would

not fail. "You are beautiful, Julia," her mother told her, "and your beauty can save us now."

But Julia couldn't bring herself to go along with her mother's plan. She thought it wrong to misrepresent her family fortunes to catch a husband for his money. Wasn't lying and false pretenses as bad as whatever Geoffrey had done?

When she tried to explain her reasons for refusing, her mother had been aghast. "You are thinking of your own happiness at a time like this? You silly girl. What do you know of happiness in marriage? Will you be happy in complete poverty? Will you be happy coming from a shunned family? The right husband can lift you back to a position of respect."

She fared no better with her father. While he was not in complete agreement with his wife's idea to send Julia to London for the season, he thought some of Julia's notions were foolish. "For most girls," he said, "love comes after marriage."

At first her mother had been patient and cajoling, trying to help Julia see the error in her reasoning. But Julia knew she could never pull off the charade in London her mother had in mind. The more fiercely Julia refused, the angrier her mother became until she came to blame Julia as much as her brother for the downfall of the family.

Julia had always been sweet and complying, a dutiful daughter, but she did have a streak of stubbornness. In the past, her ideas of decorum had always coincided with her parents' ideas. This time was different. Once Julia decided that her mother's idea was morally wrong, nothing could induce her to go along. Instead, she announced that she would hire herself out as a lady's maid.

"My son is in prison and my daughter is going into service," her father had said gloomily. "Everything I have worked for is gone."

Even Julia's promise to send them her wages did little to appease them. "A lady's maid earns a pittance!" her mother had said.

Julia hadn't answered. As became a respectful daughter, she avoided answering back. But what she was thinking was: "A lady's maid earns a pittance, but at least it is an honest pittance."

She stopped behind a hedge and looked down at the apron she wore. For a single wicked moment, she wished she had gone along with her parent's plan so she could have danced in London's finest ballrooms, worn gowns of satin and lace, and perhaps even been courted by knights and noblemen. Then she pulled herself up. How could she live a charade? And suppose she had gotten someone to propose? What would he say later to discover she was penniless, her family shamed?

How ironic that she had gone into service to avoid playing the charade her parents had demanded of her, but now that she was here, she felt just as much like an imposter.

The following morning Julia woke up early but stayed in bed until the morning bells rang and Blanche stretched herself awake. Both girls rose and dressed in silence. Julia was acutely aware that outside at the stables, Lord Guildford was waiting for her. Well, she was a maid in his house. His designs on her could not possibly be honorable. Moreover, the last thing she wanted was trouble. She needed this position, desperately.

After breakfast – Blanche and Cecilia ate in the servant's dining room and Cecilia joined her family – the three of them walked in the gardens. The air was cool, the sky unusually clear. Lady Cecilia talked about her heartache and worries. Blanche comforted her, while Julia, feeling utterly inadequate, remained silent. The merry blue of the sky seemed a mockery of Lady Cecilia's tears and heartache.

They paused to rest on a marble bench when Lord Guildford's valet approached them. "Julia, I have something for you." He handed her a sealed sheet of paper. "It is from my master, Lord Guildford," he said.

She broke the seal, aware that Lady Cecilia and Blanche were watching her. The note read:

Dear Julia,
I waited over an hour this morning in vain. Have I offended you? Can you doubt the sincerity of my request? My valet waits for an answer.
R.G.

There was a second sheet of paper as well. On it was written a poem which she recognized immediately as one of Robert Herrick's:

"One asked me where the roses grew
I bade him not go see,
But forewith bade my Julia show
A bud in either cheek.

Then Julia let me woo thee,
Thus, thus to come unto me;
And when I shall meet Thy silvery feet,
My soul I'll pour into thee."

Now, what could Julia say with both Cecilia and Blanche listening? She handed the note back to the valet. "I cannot go!" she whispered.

"I will relay your response to Lord Guildford," he said.

Julia stood still for a moment after the valet left, afraid to turn around and face Blanche and Cecilia. "What was that all about?" Cecilia asked.

"Your brother made a request of me," she said quietly, looking down at her hands, "but I refused."

"You just arrived yesterday! What did he want you do to?"

"Does it matter," Julia asked, "since I have refused him?"

A look of sad understanding came into Cecilia's face. "I see," she said. "Why have you refused him?"

"I have listened to your warnings," Julia said, "and I know you spoke the truth. I want only to fulfill my post as your lady's maid."

That night, when Blanche and Julia returned to their bedroom, Julia found a sealed letter on her pillow. "It's from him," Blanche said.

"I believe so," Julia said. She picked up the note, and without opening it, set it on the night table in the corner near her bed.

"What exactly has he asked you to do?"

"He asked me to meet him at the stables and go riding with him. But I didn't want to go. I told him I want nothing to pass between us that isn't proper between a master and a servant."

Blanche was all amazement. Then she actually laughed.

"My dear innocent Julia. Lord Guildford may have very different ideas about what is proper between a master and a servant than you have."

"Then he may need a few lessons in what is proper."

Again, Blanche laughed. "I'm sure that was the first time the great Lord Guildford has been refused. He certainly never expected to be refused by a maid in his house with a lecture on propriety. He probably has no idea what to make of you."

Blanche undressed for bed, and Julia did the same. She left the note where it was, the seal intact.

Blanche was in bed with the sheets pulled up to her chin when she said, "Don't you want to know what he has written?"

"No. First he made his sister miserable, forcing a man on her that she doesn't want. Now he plans to make me miserable. I wish he would leave me alone and never look at me again."

Blanche studied Julia for what felt like a very long time.

"What?" Julia asked, alarmed.

"I've risen this far," Blanche said, "because I've learned how to read people's faces. Yours is hard to read, Julia. You keep your secrets well hidden, but I can see in your face there are things you are not telling."

With that, she blew out the night candle and they were in darkness.

When Blanche and Julia left the room the following morning, the note remained where it was, unopened. By midmorning, Julia's curiosity got to her. She revised her plan. She would return to her room during a free moment, read his note, and then destroy it. Her chance came later that afternoon, when Lady Cecilia was busy at her writing desk and Blanche fell asleep on the divan in the adjoining room. Excusing herself, she returned to their room and quickly broke the seal.

Dear Julia,
"Let me not to the marriage of true minds admit impediments."
I beg you only to tell me how I have offended you or what I may alter in myself to win the time to tell you of my feelings. I am yours faithfully,
Robert

Julia sat still for a moment as an idea came to her. She went to search for a pen and wrote:

Lord Guildford,
You ask me to tell you how you have offended, or I would never presume to criticize one so far above my station. I can never love or want a man who inflicts such misery upon his sister. Marriage is a sacred state and not to be forced upon another. One who

uses his sister in such a way can never have honorable designs upon a humble lady's maid such as,
    Julia

She sealed the note and took it to the butler's pantry. Her purpose gave her a new boldness. When she knocked on the door, Mr. Ames called, "Enter."

She entered and curtseyed. "Forgive my intrusion," she said. "His lordship has made me a written request, and I have responded. Will you please give him my reply?"

He took the note from her. He didn't seem at all surprised. "I will see that he gets this."

"Thank you, sir."

She returned to find Lady Cecilia pacing angrily and Blanche trying to calm her. "But you heard the commands," Cecilia said, "from my own uncle! I will be compelled tomorrow to read the settlements and sign them by evening! There is no hope for me!"

"There must be hope," Blanche said.

"There is none! My uncle has sworn that the wedding will be celebrated before the end of the month." She clenched her fists and said, "How I hate them! And how I hate how powerless I am to stand up to them!"

"Shh–" Blanche cautioned. From the corridor came the sound of approaching footsteps. Then came a knock at the door.

Lady Cecilia took a moment to collect herself, and then said, "Enter."

The door opened and in came Mr. Ames, Lord Guildford's butler. "His lordship has had a change of heart. He bids me tell you that, if you wish it, he will tell Sir Ruthven that the family will decline his proposal. In exchange, he asks that you promise you will never marry against his wishes–"

Cecilia jumped up. "Can it be true?" She looked at Blanche. "I've never known my brother to change his mind, once he made it up. What can this mean?"

Mr. Ames said, "Your brother says that he will discuss it further with you at dinner. You can tell him then whether you will agree not to marry against his wishes."

"Can I see him now? What is he doing?"

"He has a four o'clock appointment with the vicar on his southern estates. After that, he would be pleased to see you."

Julia was glad nobody was paying the slightest attention to her. She, too, was in complete amazement, but she alone knew why he had changed his mind. Or at least she thought she knew.

That night, Blanche placed a night candle beside Lady Cecilia's bed. Julia and Blanche returned to their own bedroom. There on Julia's pillow, was a sealed note. As before, she had no wish to open the note in front of Blanche, but this time her curiosity won out. She broke open the seal and read:

Dear Julia,

Do you see how you rule my heart? Do you see how much I am willing to do for your sake? Your day off is Tuesday. I will be waiting for you early in the morning, at the stables, to take you riding. Please do not disappoint me again. Instead, you can make me

the happiest of men. Yours to command always is,
  Robert G.

She folded the letter and tucked it into her waistband. She knew Blanche was watching her while pretending not to, so she said, "Lord Guildford is a determined man."

"And he always gets what he wants," said Blanche.

The following morning, Blanche and Julia entered Lady Cecilia's chambers to find her at her dressing table, staring at the neat array of combs and brushes and cologne bottles.

"How do you do this morning, my lady?" Blanche asked.

"I'm delighted, of course, with my brother's change of heart. It is a relief not to have to deal with Sir Ruthven's proposals. But Julia, come here a moment. I have something to ask you."

Julia felt Blanche watching her. "Yes, my lady?"

"My brother said something quite strange. Perhaps you can clear up the mystery for me. He said I have you to thank for his change of heart. Now what on earth did he mean by that?"

"Your brother asked me why I've been cold to him and why I have shunned his advances. I gave him reasons, including the vast difference in our stations. He asked how he could mend his behavior to win my favor. I told him I could never think kindly of a man who compelled his sister to marry a man she despised."

Cecilia was deeply astonished. Julia glanced at Blanche and saw that she, too, was astonished.

"You did that for me?" Cecilia asked.

"I honestly never expected him to act upon my command."

"Indeed," said Cecilia softly. "He acts upon nobody's command."

"Perhaps," said Blanche, "it is because he is not accustomed to having to work so hard to get what he wants from a maid."

"I am afraid for you, Julia," Cecilia said. "You are so sweet and good, you don't have the cunning necessary to best my brother at the game he wants to play with you. You have done me a favor, so I will protect you as best I can."

In that drowsy moment just before awakening, Julia stretched herself in her bed, smelling the powdery scent of the linen sheets. She also smelled something herbal which reminded her of the woodlands behind her parents' house in Worthing. She had been dreaming something pleasant but she couldn't remember what it was. She expected to open her eyes and see the crinole curtains of her bedroom windows in Worthing and smell the cook downstairs preparing the family breakfast. Her mother would already be downstairs supervising the preparations, and her father would be at his writing desk.

She heard someone moving around the room and her eyes sprang open. For one bewildered moment her mind was a complete blank. Then she remembered where she was.

"You certainly are a sound sleeper," said Blanche. "I thought I'd have to reach over and pinch you to wake you up."

"I'm awake," Julia assured her. She stretched and reached for the dressing gown folded at the foot of her bed. Blanche was already dressed and splashing water on her face from the basin. Julia heard the faint ringing of bells at the end of the corridor. She knew she had to hurry.

"I'm going now," Blanche announced. "I'll see you at breakfast."

Julia was out of bed, washing at the basin, then pulling on a fresh chemise, trying to shake herself free from drowsiness. When she was dressed, her hair braided and tucked into her cap, her apron smoothed in place, she gave herself a quick check in the mirror.

She was on the backstairs when she heard the sound of heavy boot steps coming toward her. She stopped to listen on the landing between the first and second floors, her heartbeat quickening.

Then, around the corner, came Lord Guildford. He stopped at the sight of her, apparently as surprised as she was. "Julia," he said.

She couldn't move, so taken was she by his smile. "My lord," she said, then, remembering herself, she bobbed a curtsey.

"I've been watching for you. I've wanted to talk to you, to make sure you will meet me on Tuesday."

"But—"

"But what, Julia?"

"But nothing is really possible between us."

"What on earth do you mean? Everything is possible. Anything is possible."

She felt confused. "But I am a lady's maid, nothing more. And you are–"

"Let us forget such differences, my lovely Julia. What do they matter, really?"

His face was so earnest, his smile so sincere, that she was almost able to believe him.

"Why then," she asked, "would you send me one of Robert Herrick's verses?"

He blinked, startled. "Because it is beautiful. Because he writes about a lovely girl named Julia. I take it you do not care for the verse of Robert Herrick?"

"Indeed, I do not."

"Oh, Julia. How little you understand."

He stepped forward until he was close enough to touch her. To look into his face she had to tip her head back. He made her feel reckless and daring, as if anything really were possible.

"But," she said, "you don't know anything about me, or about my family."

"I know what I need to know. I can look at you, Julia, and see that you are a girl of rare character." He touched her chin and tipped her head back so she was looking directly at him. "But if I might say so, you are perhaps too serious."

She blinked, astonished at this. When she'd refused, on principal, to go to London in borrowed clothes in search of a wealthy husband, her mother had said, "Julia, you are too serious. You take everything, including yourself, too seriously. Sometimes we do what we need to do without thinking too precisely about it."

"You are young," he said, "and lovely and can have whatever you want from life. Why not take it? Are you happy as you are, as a simple lady's maid? Or do you want more?"

"Of course I want more." Or did she? Wouldn't wanting more have led her to London in borrowed clothes?

Her reaction seemed to please him. "If you want something more," he said, "take it."

Was it as simple as that? He wanted her, she could see that in the way he looked at her. And she certainly wanted him. Perhaps it didn't matter that she was a lady's maid, the daughter of a small town mayor.

"I will be waiting," he said, "on Tuesday."

Tuesday morning dawned misty and gray. Julia peered past the curtains, wondering if it would rain. Northward the skies were stormy, but southward the skies were clear. As she dressed, she had the uncomfortable feeling that Blanche wasn't really asleep. Blanche would guess easily enough why she was in such a hurry to leave today, her first day off. Thankfully Blanche wasn't asking any questions. She spared Julia that embarrassment.

Once Julia was out of the room, she walked slowly and deliberately downstairs and out a side door toward the stables, trying to calm her racing pulse. She was frightened and anxious. At the same time, she felt brave and daring. Who would have thought possible what she was about to do? A voice in her head told her that this could be the happiest day of her life. Another voice was whispering that she was a fool, that she would be cautious, that she should take nothing for granted.

But when she saw him she forgot all caution. He was leaning against the trunk of a gnarled oak just in front of the stables. He stood up straight and watched her approach, his smile full of admiration. How different he was from any other man she had ever known. His confidence came close to arrogance: he had been born to rule, and he knew it.

"Julia, you've come." He reached for her hands. His touch was a shock which she felt all through her being. She knew, from his tension and heightened color, that he was feeling the exact same excitement.

"I was afraid–" she broke off shyly. Her fears seemed absurd now that she was with him. He had made it clear, from the first moment he had seen her on the road leading to Guildford Manor, that he was a man of honor and would never treat her as an inferior.

"You don't have to be afraid of me," he said. He put his arms around her, pulling her close. She melted into him. His arms tightened around her and his lips brushed against her hair.

She believed he was right. She didn't have to be afraid of him. He had promised her that anything was possible between them, and she believed him.

"Let's get away from here," he said, his voice low and husky. "I have horses ready."

"Where will we go?"

"This is beautiful country, Julia. I want to show it to you."

He led her to a dappled mare and helped her

mount. He swung himself on his own mount and flicked the reins. He turned to make sure she was following, and then cantered off to a trail which led through a grove of oaks. As they set off, she realized it had been many months since she'd been on a horse. Until her father's fall from grace, he had kept a small stable with a half dozen horses. She loved to ride. She loved the fresh air and the feel of the wind in her hair.

He was right, the country was lovely, with lush green hills and hedges of hawthorn and brier. The hills were sown thickly with gold cup flowers, the moss on the rocks a bright, dazzling green. The clouds were breaking up, showing patches of blue.

They came to a narrow creek and crossed a bridge which was nothing more than a half dozen planks and a crude handrail. In the distance was a village, a cluster of thatched cottages around a white-steepled church.

Each time he looked at her, she smiled. She felt a giggle rise in her throat. She hadn't felt this happy in months. Perhaps she had never in her life been this lightheaded and joyful. She felt completely free, as wild as the flowers scattered along the trail, as if all her cares and all the troubles she and her family had gone through during the past months would fade away.

She wanted to look at him all the time, and was happiest when he rode ahead so she could admire the shape of his shoulders.

As a child she had invented stories of knights and dragons to entertain her family. When she had gotten a little older, she had amused her brother by making up plays and acting all the roles herself. But even

Julia, with all the powers of her creative mind, had never even imagined that such an incredibly handsome nobleman, the catch of all England, would fall in love with her.

"We'll go to the top of that hill," Guildford said, pointing. "From there we will have the best view of the entire valley."

He knew the way through the meadow and marshy bogs, moving with the complete confidence of one who had ridden this way many times. "I am taking you to my favorite spot in all the world," he told her.

As they left the main trail and went into the wilds, her fears returned. Young girls simply did not go off alone with men this way, unescorted. Julia's parents would die of fright if they knew what she was doing. They wouldn't believe it of her, for she had always been the soul of propriety. But what choice did she have? She was a lady's maid, and not exactly in a position to demand an escort, nor to demand to know in advance what he intended to say to her. She reminded herself that she had no reason to fear him–he had promised as much, after all–but her heart felt weak and fluttery.

As they neared the top of the hill, the breeze grew stronger, rustling the grass and the leaves of the trees in a low, comforting whisper. Lord Guildford was riding beside her now. As they came up alongside an elderly birch, its bark as white as a bleached summer frock, he reached for her reins, then dismounted and tied both their horses to a low hanging branch. He came to help her down, guiding her to the ground.

When her feet touched the ground, he steadied her, his arms around her. She felt his warmth and could smell the faint scent of jasmine that clung to his clothing, mixed with the scent of horses and leather.

"Julia," he whispered. "I have so much to tell you, so much to ask you, to talk to you about-" he paused, bringing up his hand to the nape of her neck and stroking her hair where it was tucked into her braid. He touched her chin and tipped her head back, and then his lips were on hers. His kiss was so tender and gentle that she could make no protest.

She wanted to hear what he would say, but she was drawn into his kiss, fearing she could never summon the strength to pull away from him.

He tightened his grip around her back, pulling her closer to him, crushing her breasts against his chest. At the same time the nature of his kiss changed, deepening. Tiny shivers ran through her and she pushed herself closer to him as if to absorb his warmth, to calm her trembling limbs.

He scooped her up in his arms as easily as if she were a weightless doll. He walked a few paces away, to where the grass was thickest, scattered with dandelions and gold cup flowers. Still cradling her, he sat, holding her in his lap.

The movement brought her back to her senses. "But-" she started to say, but his lips were on hers again.

He pulled back just enough to whisper, "Julia, I knew from the moment I saw you that you were meant to be mine. You felt it, too. I know you did."

She shook her head and wanted to tell him no, she had never imagined he could really love her. It had seemed impossible, the kind of thing that happened only in fairytale fantasies.

He lowered his head and kissed her neck. The

sensation made her weak with pleasure. His touch consumed her, taking her breath away, making the world around her disappear. Her feeling was one of complete surrender. She surprised herself by running her hands over his shoulders and back, reveling in the feel of his muscles hardened beneath her hands. He responded by kissing her more deeply still, his hands moving in circles across her back.

Yes, she thought, this was inevitable. They were meant for each other. It was impossible that anyone else could stir such feelings in her and cause her to throw her head back shamelessly as his lips moved ever lower, to the ribbon that laced her bodice. His hands were encircling her waist, then he moved one hand higher until he was stroking her breast. The sensation was maddening. As if he sensed her urgency, he tugged at the ribbon, loosening her bodice so that he could slide his hand inside.

He laid her down gently and pushed the material of her bodice downward. The sensations as he touched her were so shocking, so pleasurable that she felt the tremors all through her body, down her spine, making her limbs weak.

Then one of his hands was on her thigh, sliding upward beneath her skirt. When he reached the spot between her legs, the place where she had always imagined no man but her husband would ever touch, she stiffened, all her earlier fright returning.

"No," she said, gasping for breath. She didn't know how to address him. He was still Lord Guildford to her, but the formality of his title was a startling contrast to the intimacy with which he now touched her. "We must stop. This is too soon, please."

"Too soon? Each hour I have waited for you seemed like a year. I feel like I've waited longer for you than I've ever waited for anyone."

It took a moment for the meaning of his words to make sense to her. This wasn't what he should be saying. "You wanted to talk to me," she said, hearing the plea in her voice. "You had things to ask me."

"Yes, Julia, we have much to discuss. I will change your life, I promise. You were meant for better, that's easy enough to see. You don't want to spend your life as a lady's maid, do you?"

"No, of course not."

"Julia, I know so little about you. I want to hear your entire story, how you came to take the position in my house, what you did before. I want to know what you want, Julia, and whatever it is, I will see that you get your heart's desire."

She stiffened and covered her breasts. But this wasn't right. He wasn't supposed to be talking this way. She felt uncomfortable with her clothes disheveled, and her hair falling over her back and shoulders. This just wasn't the way it was supposed to happen.

He touched her cheek, then took her hand and kissed it.

"There is something I want to give you."

He took a small casket from his vest pocket. She stared at him, her heart pounding.

He said, "The first time I saw the deep blue of your eyes, I thought of this sapphire. I wanted to bring you a gift as a token of my love. I want to give you something blue, to match your eyes. This was my grandmother's, and then my mother's. No one else but you can really wear a jewel this color. I want you to have it."

His mother's sapphire! Would he really give her an heirloom? She was almost afraid to look down at the casket, which he now held open. Inside was a small brooch with smooth blue stone set amid a dozen tiny diamonds set in a floral pattern. When he moved the brooch, the white star clinging like a spider to the stone moved as well.

"It's a star sapphire," he explained. "Will you wear it?"

She swallowed. Lady's maids didn't wear such fine jewelry. She wanted to know what he intended, what this meant, but she was afraid to ask. "I don't know what to say," she said truthfully.

His arms were around her again and he drew her head to his chest. "There will be plenty of time for talk, later. I wanted you to know that my regard for you is real. Now I want to kiss you, Julia. Look at me."

She kept her face pressed to his chest and shook her head. He had said his regard was real, but that wasn't enough. "Tell me now what you have to talk to me about," she said, humiliated to force him to talk this way, but not knowing what else to do.

He touched her cheek and then brushed his lips against her temple. "Trust me, my Julia. I know I haven't earned your trust yet, but I will. You'll see that you have nothing to fear."

"What do you mean?" This time she pulled free from him and moved a few inches away, pulling her clothing back into shape as best she could. He was close enough so that he could touch her easily, but she didn't want his hands on her, not yet, not until she understood what he was about. A fear, like an icy wind, was creeping up on her, making her shudder. She tied the ribbons of her bodice.

"All right, Julia, if you want to settle our arrangements first, that's fine with me." Bits of twigs and grass clung to the gray velvet of his waistcoat. She was tempted to reach out and brush off his shoulders, but she remained still.

"Arrangements?" she asked. She thought the word oddly businesslike. Still, if he said the magical words, none of the rest would matter.

"You seem to doubt me," he said, "although I can't imagine why. You can have, of your own, an annual income of two hundred pounds a year."

Two hundred pounds a year! The sum stunned her. That was enough money to restore her family to the life they were accustomed to, but she still didn't understand what he was offering her. She felt hopelessly inexperienced. She looked down at the brooch, wondering if he could, after all, be talking of marriage settlements.

"Or," he said, "if you prefer, I can set you up in a shop of your own. You may choose where. An accessories shop in London? A gallery of some sort? Do you have a preference?"

She couldn't look at him. She pretended to concentrate on shredding a blade of grass, willing her hands to stop trembling. Now she understood. Julia felt a sickness low in her stomach. Her parents would never accept a shilling which she had earned as a kept mistress, nor would she ever dare offer it to them. Perhaps he thought he was honoring her, but Julia found the offer degrading and insulting.

She had been told that she was naive, full of wide-eyed fantasies, and now she felt like a complete fool.

Anyone else would have known what he was all about. He probably thought his intentions had been perfectly clear.

"Julia," he said softly, "how do you answer? Are you pleased with my offer?"

She swallowed, waiting until she dared trust her voice. Still, she couldn't look at him when she said, "I cannot accept your offer." Her words came out in a hoarse whisper.

She picked up the casket and handed it back to him, understanding now that he had offered her the brooch the way a man offers jewels to his mistress. "Please take this back. I cannot accept gifts from you. Now I would like you to take me back to the house."

"Julia, I don't think you have understood me. You may name your terms. I promise to give you whatever is in my power."

"Is that a promise?" She looked directly at him.

"Of course. I must have you, Julia, and I will. Tell me what you want and you will have it."

"You promise this, and you are a man who keeps his promises?"

"I assure you that I am."

She may as well say the words. She wanted to test his reaction, to see how far astray her fantasies and imaginings had led her. "Then I would like you to marry me."

For a moment his face registered no response, then his eyes grew larger and he stared at her as if she were a complete stranger. Yes, she had managed to shock him.

"That's impossible," he said, his lips barely moving.

"Is it? You promised to do whatever was in your

power."

"Marriage is not in my power, Julia. I will inherit an earldom. I will be a peer of the realm. You know what the standards are in marriage for a man such as myself."

She wanted to cry, to rage at him, to call him vile names, but pride stopped her. She felt like a complete fool. She stood up. "If you are a man of honor, as you claim to be, you will honor my request and return me to the house at once."

He rose as well, and stared at her for a long moment, evidently weighing her words, looking as if he were trying to understand a mysterious riddle. She felt she had delivered her speech well, keeping her pride intact.

"Julia," he said, stepping closer. His nearness confused her, as it always did. But she was not going to let him get the better of her. If he wanted a paid mistress, he could woo Blanche or any of the girls of the villages who would have him. She turned and walked toward their horses. Untying her mare from the tree, she held the reins and pulled herself up. Once she sat atop the horse, she looked at him. He followed her and stood a few paces away. From this vantage point she could look down on him, a satisfying sensation. Later she would feel her rage and disappointment. For now she wanted only to show a pride and reserve befitting a great lady.

She sensed he was about to say something more, so she waited, feeling that her life depended on his next words. All he said was, "I'll take you back. Think about, it Julia. That's all I ask.

Guildford mounted his horse and led the way back down the hill, astounded by her response. It simply hadn't occurred to him that she would refuse his offer, particularly given how easily he'd been able to arouse her. On the surface she was all sweetness and decorum with a seriousness which, in a less beautiful girl, would strike him as down right priggish–but from his first sight of her, he suspected that beneath her perfectly cool exterior, she had a sensuous nature. Her response to his kisses confirmed his belief that once awakened, she would take particular delight in sensuous pleasures. Yes, all in all, he still believed that once he won her over she would make the perfect mistress: sweet and complying.

He certainly hadn't expected her to ask for marriage, of all things. When she'd first stopped him, wanting to know what he was offering, he'd been taken aback, disappointed in her. That was the sort of thing he would expect from a girl like Blanche. He hadn't expected Julia to toy with him, or try to bargain with him. His only idea was that her demand for marriage was a way of holding out for more, hoping for a better offer.

He listened to the clipping of horse hooves behind him and the rustling of shrubs. He slowed to let her catch up. When he heard her own horse slow down as well, he stopped and turned around. She pulled her horse to a stop, looking at him with something almost like fright.

He took just a few tentative steps toward her, not

enough to increase her alarm. "If I have somehow offended you, I assure you that I meant no offense. I meant only to make an offer worthy of you. My offer stands. You have my heart and whatever is mine to give. You have only to command me."

He watched her reaction carefully, surprised by what he saw. The corners of her mouth pinched downward as if she would cry. A look of almost unbearable sadness came over her lovely face. "I just want to go back," she said. "That is all I want."

Guildford did not understand this girl at all. The last thing he had expected today was to bring such a look of heartbreaking pain to that beautiful face. He had thought to shower her with love and adoration and presents.

He turned forward and began moving again, listening to the sounds of her behind him. What a mystery she was, behaving as if he had paid her a grave insult. Her tearful disappointment left him with one conclusion: she hadn't been bargaining at all. She had genuinely expected a proposal of marriage. The idea astonished him. If she had expected marriage, then she was indeed a little innocent, far more so than he could ever have suspected.

The other thing he never expected was for her to hand back his mother's sapphire as if it were made of worthless glass. The brooch had been in his family for three generations, since his grandmother married his grandfather. He had chosen the gift with care. The first time he had seen her on the road, her eyes had reminded him of the sapphire. The jewel was the same deeply glowing blue. The jewel itself reminded him of her as well. There was nothing ostentatious about the brooch, its loveliness came from its simple perfection and the sense of light coming from within.

He turned again and stopped his horse. She stopped also. He felt entirely ungallant to press on when she was clearly so distressed, but he could not leave matters as they were. Feeling he needed to regain the upper hand, he said, "You demand much, if you expected a proposal of marriage."

His words had the effect he intended. She was flustered. "My lord, I had no such expectation–"

"I believe you did."

"I thought you wanted to–" she broke off and looked down. Then, lifting her chin bravely, she turned her magnificent eyes to him. "I thought you wanted to talk to me. I thought you wanted to learn more about me, to find out if I am a girl you can love."

Love? So she was a romantic. He should have expected this. He wanted to smile, but was afraid of appearing condescending. She was so serious, so earnest. Even after the events of this past hour, he could not resist teasing her.

"Love, Julia? What is love? The great poets tell us that love is not hereafter. It is present mirth making present laughter. You do laugh, don't you? Sometimes?" He inclined his head, pretending an earnestness to match her own. "Or perhaps you dislike all poets, not just Herrick. Too much merriment and passion."

He smiled at her flustered expression. Without waiting for a response, he turned forward and spurred his horse lightly. He had no doubt now, from the way she'd looked at him, that he could tempt her again into his arms. It would just be a matter of time before they could settle on an arrangement pleasing to them both. Perhaps she would talk to the worldly-wise Blanche, who would laugh at her expectations and tell her that she was fortunate to have so splendid an offer. In a week, or even less, she would respond differently to his proposals.

The sad irony was that he *had* planned to talk to her. Talk hadn't been the first item on his agenda, naturally, but he'd fully intended to learn her story. Who was she? Where was she from? He could guess easily enough that this was her first position in service, and he knew from the way she spoke that she came from a better class family. She had read Herrick. Her writing was neat and she spelled correctly.

From her response when he'd accused her of being too serious, he suspected he'd stumbled on a truth about her. She needed to learn to relax and enjoy the good things in life. This morning, for example, was perfect for lovemaking. The air was warm and fragrant, the hillside lovely. One day–and he hoped the day would come soon–he would teach her to set aside her seriousness and enjoy life's pleasures.

Julia, for her part, wanted only to get back to the house, so she could get away from him. It took all her energy to keep her countenance calm, to hide her rage and turmoil. She wanted to be alone, so she could adjust to her disappointment.

At long last they approached the stables. Two stable boys, busy brushing the horses, looked up as they approached. She guessed from the way the two stable boys watched them that before long the entire household would know how she had spent her free morning. Blanche would find out, and even Lady Cecilia. How would she hide her disappointment and not let any of them know what a fool she had been?

She stopped just outside the stables. She didn't want to follow Guildford inside. She slid to the ground and tossed the reins to the stable boy who came forward to meet her. Then she picked up her skirts, and without looking once at Guildford, ran around to the back gardens toward the orchards where she knew she could find a private place hidden from view of the house.

It was her day off, so she could remain outside, by herself. She badly needed time alone, to bring order back to her thoughts and tranquility back to her mind. She found a shady place to sit on a soft bed of old leaves. All around her was the sweet and uplifting scent of apple blossoms. The orchards were so vast that Julia guessed dozens of people would be employed to pick the apples. The smell of apple blossoms reminded her of last year's apple picking with her family in Worthing. They had four large apple trees in the yard, enough to fill dozens of baskets. For weeks the kitchen smelled of sweet apples as the cook and two hired kitchen maids baked fresh tarts for the Brandon' table and canned the rest, lining the jars on the pantry shelves. How long ago it all seemed!

For lunch she ate fruit from the orchards. After

she ate, she found a place to sit. She closed her eyes and, despite herself, remembered how Lord Guildford's body had felt pressed up against hers, how exciting it had been to be cradled in his arms. Just remembering how he had kissed and fondled her sent a warm glowing sensation down her limbs. Resisting him would not be easy. Well, she told herself wryly, that's why it's called temptation.

She would simply have to remember herself. From now on she would take care that he never guess, from the expression of her eyes or her demeanor, the effect he had on her. She would hold herself proudly, and eventually he would understand that what he had wanted from her was impossible.

When she could see from the slant of the sun that the time had come for her to return, she brushed off her skirts and headed resolutely to the house.

She found Blanche in the servants' dining room with the others. They were just sitting down to supper when Julia came in. She smiled at Blanche. In response, Blanche gave her a look she could not read, something between understanding and cynicism, which Julia assumed meant everyone was talking about her morning ride with Lord Guildford.

She ate in silence, avoiding looking at anyone at the table. When the spiced meat and bread cooked with herbs was placed on the table, her mouth watered and she realized how hungry she was. After all, all she'd had all afternoon were a few apples.

After supper, she and Blanche were on their way up the backstairs to Cecilia's room when Blanche said, "Come here a minute," and pulled her into a private alcove. "I need a word with you."

Once they were out of the main staircase, Blanche said, "I knew there was something you weren't telling, so I did some investigating."

Blanche's clipped tone sent a shiver down Julie's back.

"Your father," said Blanche, "is John Brandon, the former mayor of Worthing. Your name isn't Dale at all. Now I know why you give yourself airs."

Airs? Julia's shock gave way to genuinely hurt feelings. Was that how Blanche saw her, when really, she was simply treading carefully so she wouldn't make a misstep?

"So," Blanche went on, "you have a university-educated brother, and you're the daughter of a mayor."

"I am the daughter of a *former* mayor, not a mayor. There's a world of difference. Maybe you don't know the entire story, but my father–"

"I know the entire story. I know more than you think. And Lady Cecilia knows, too. Naturally she wanted to know your connection to the Brandons."

So word of her father's shame and her family's scandal had indeed traveled this far.

"Lady Cecilia said you're to go to her right away after supper. She'll be waiting for you."

Julia knocked softly on Cecilia's door. When Lady Cecilia called "Enter," Julia opened the door and stepped inside. Blanche, who had followed a few paces behind her, also entered and closed the door behind them.

51

Julia expected Cecilia to be as angry and as cold as Blanche. She was thus taken completely by surprise when Cecilia, who was seated on the fringed stool in front of her dressing table, turned to face her, her face glowing and alive as if lit by torches from within.

"Come in, Julia," she said. "Sit here." She pointed to the stool in front of her.

Julia sat down, even more startled when Cecilia took her hands and said, "Your name is Julia Brandon. Your father is John Brandon and your brother is Geoffrey."

Julia felt confused. She suspected there was a connection she should be making just then, but in her nervousness all she could think to say was, "I'm so sorry I lied. I was afraid that if anyone knew of my family's shame, I'd never get a post. You see–"

Cecilia cut her off, raising her hand to stop her. She smiled, her expression soft and gentle. "I know all about what happened to your family. You see, the man I love is your brother, Geoffrey."

This stopped Julia cold. She blinked.

"Geoffrey–? *You*–but–?" Julia realized she was stammering.

Cecilia's smile broadened. "I suppose I'm not the only one with a handsome and devilish brother."

"But how did you meet? How did it happen?"

"I met Geoffrey when I was in London. He came to a ball given by the Earl of Sunderly. He'd met the earl's cousin at the university. My brother caught us together–" Cecilia broke off, giggling shyly.

"Don't mince words, my lady," Blanche said. "Tell the whole truth, so Julia understands."

"He caught us in a, well, shall we say,

embarrassing situation."

"He caught them in the hay," Blanche said.

Julie actually gasped. "The *hay*?"

"It's an expression, my little innocent," said Blanche, "and perhaps where you were this morning as well."

Before Julia could protest, Blanche said, "Naturally, Lord Guildford met him in a duel."

"Lord *Guildford* met him?" Julia said. "I thought Geoffrey dueled with someone named Lord Howard."

"That is my uncle Jervis," said Cecilia. "My uncle was the one who challenged him, but Robert was the one who met him. Robert would never let my uncle, who is so much older, fight a duel. Robert is much better with a sword."

"Such foolishness!" Julia said. "One of them could have been killed!"

"Robert was content to knock Geoffrey's sword out of his hand, injuring his arm, and pinning him to the ground." Cecilia drew herself up proudly and said, "Even pinned to the ground with a sword near his throat, Geoffrey would not promise to stay away from me. Robert accused Geoffrey of seducing me to get his hands on my dowry. My uncle charged him with abducting me."

"So that was the charge," Julie said. "I thought he was involved in something like a gambling quarrel." Julia found it difficult to adjust to the idea that the man Cecilia was in love with was her brother Geoffrey. Once she got over her original shock, it occurred to her that Cecilia and her brother had much in common. Both were highly passionate, and both were generous. The adjustment she had most

53

trouble making was that Lord Guildford and Geoffrey had dueled. She could imagine her hot-headed brother dueling, but she simply could not imagine Lord Guildford angry enough to lift his sword with the intention of causing injury.

"I hardly know what to say, or think," Julia said.

"Let me kiss your cheek," Cecilia said, and she did just that. "Now that I know you are Geoffrey's own sister, how much dearer you are to me! I see the resemblance now, of course. You both have the same fine features and deep blue eyes. You must have reminded me of Geoffrey when I interviewed you, which is why I took to you right away. The best part, is that you can help me send letters to your brother. All you have to do is tuck one of mine in the next letter you send. And you are going to write to your brother soon, is that not right?"

"But if Blanche figured out who my father is," Julia said. "Won't the others, too, if they start inquiring?"

"Blanche figured it out and told me. Nobody else knows. It will be perfectly safe for you to send my letters. You will do it, won't you?"

Well, why shouldn't she? If Blanche figured out who she was so easily, it was only a matter of time before that butler, and Lord Guildford, and his uncles found out as well and she'd no doubt be cast out of the house. It occurred to her, though, in light of what happened that morning, that being expelled from the house might not be the worst thing.

"I suppose I will," Julia said.

"Good. Now, there is one other thing I must talk to you about. I must warn you about my brother. You see, I'm afraid that in your innocence you will believe he is capable of loving when he really has no heart at all. I never thought I'd say this about my own brother. Until last year, I thought he was the sweetest, dearest, most loving brother in the world. But the past year has brought so many changes that I can't help conclude-"

"My lady, really-" Blanche interrupted.

"Are you still tempted to defend him, Blanche? Even after all that has happened?"

"But you know you exaggerate."

"I'll admit that until last year, I adored him. But his behavior since has been horrid, and I really do have to warn Julia." To Julia, she said, "Never forget this. He always gets whatever girl he wants. He is fully aware of the powers of his smile."

"You don't have to warn me," said Julia. "I've already made up my mind to stay away from him. Now that I know he has caused the ruin of my family, I am doubly resolved to keep our relationship entirely formal."

"What about this morning?" Blanche asked.

"Nothing happened this morning," Julia said. Then she remembered what had happened, and she felt herself growing warm with embarrassment. "I truly hate lying," she said. "I don't know why I even try. Yes, something happened, but I got away from him, and I plan to stay away."

Blanche was looking at her closely, assessing her. What she wanted to say to Blanche was: You can have him. But she was afraid that saying such a thing would be to give herself airs.

"I don't believe you will stay away from him," Blanche said.

"Indeed," Cecilia said, "staying away from him

may not be so easy, Julia. Once my brother wants something, nothing stops him. And it is clear he wants you."

"But I will stay away from him!"

"My brother is what they call an epicure. He must always have the best of everything, the finest wine, the best horses, the prettiest girls."

"I am not a thing to be bought and sold, like a bottle of wine or fine horse," Julia said.

Blanche said nothing more until later that evening, when she and Julia were in their beds. She looked at Julia and said, "You're fooling yourself, you know. You are in love with him."

With that, she blew out the candle.

All three of them–Blanche, Julia, and Cecilia–were awakened by a light knock at Cecilia's door. Instantly Blanche was out of bed, pulling on her dressing gown. Julia did the same. By the time they entered Cecilia's room, Cecilia was standing in her dressing gown by the door, holding a letter.

"John, the footman, brought it," she whispered excitedly. "It is from Geoffrey." She sat on the bed and broke the seal, read the letter, then handed it to Blanche and Julia, so they could see it as well:

Dearest Cecilia,
I have found a barrister willing to lay my appeal before the magistrate. But I need two things: A letter signed in your own hand and sealed with your own seal swearing that I never abducted you, or did

anything against your will. I also need whatever coins you can spare. I haven't enough money to pay the barrister, and as you know my last attempt to secure funds did not turn out well. I remain yours faithfully forever,

Geoffrey

Cecilia came alive at this. "Oh! If Geoffrey can get out of prison! If he can clear his name. Think of it!" She folded the letter and hid it away in a drawer of her dressing table.

"But," said Blanche, "how on earth will we get money to him? It's hard enough to send letters!"

Cecilia sat heavily on the bed. "There must be a way."

"I will do it," Julia said. They both turned to look at her.

"You?" said Cecilia. "How?"

"I will go visit him in London. I'll say my father is ill and I need emergency leave for a few days to go home. I sent home my advance wages. I can take Geoffrey that money, and the letters from you that he needs."

"That will not work," said Blanche. "Lord Guildford will insist upon sending an escort, who will see immediately that your father is not sick."

"But my father *is* sick. He was injured when he fell from a horse."

"When? There is no new injury. There is no emergency. An escort taking you home will see immediately that your parents were not expecting you."

"Then I will have to leave without telling

anyone."

"But how will you get home?" Cecilia cried.

"I will walk. I walked here. If I leave one morning before dawn, and if you can hide my absence, I can be home by midmorning, before anyone knows I'm gone."

"I think that can work," Cecilia said. "If we can figure out how to come up with enough money for you to hire a coach to London, you could be all the way to Newcastle Prison before anyone here even realizes you are gone. But how would I ever be able to repay you?"

"What repayment would be necessary? It is my brother in prison, my family that was ruined. After he was in prison, he got into other trouble as well, something about falling in with a band of thieves, but getting his name cleared of the charges brought by your family will be a start."

"There was no other trouble," said Cecilia. "The story that he fell in with thieves is completely false!"

"Not completely," said Blanche.

"It is all exaggerated, and you know it!" To Julia, Cecilia said, "Geoffrey's friends tried to smuggle money in to him so he could bribe the guards. When he was found with the money, he was accused of stealing. My uncle, I believe, had a hand in helping to fabricate that story."

"But why?" Julia cried, "Why would your uncle do something so unjust?"

"To keep Geoffrey out of the way until I could be safely married. After a slight pause, she added: "My uncles are concerned because a lot of money is involved. My dowry is a large one."

Then Blanche startled both Julia and Cecilia by

saying, "I will go, too. It isn't safe for a girl to be walking such a long way by herself."

"I can't have you both leave!" Cecilia said. "How will I explain it? The two of us can cover up for Julia's absence, at least a while."

"I've seen more of the world than either of you," said Blanche, "and I don't see how Julia can get to London on her own."

"I'll be all right," Julia said. "I'll leave at the first light of dawn. I'll be home within three hours." She spoke with more bravado than she felt, particularly when she remembered the way Lord Guildford's friends had been ready to make sport of her when they found her on the road alone. "Then I'll figure out how to hire a coach."

"A girl, alone, in a coach, to London," Blanche said. "What will the coach driver say when you ask him to take you to Newcastle Prison?"

"First I just need to get home," said Julia, "with Lady Cecilia's letters. Then my parents will help me figure out how to get the letters and some money to Geoffrey."

Cecilia went to her dressing table and opened a drawer. "I have five pounds of my own, but no other money I can get to."

She handed the satin pouch filled with coins to Cecilia. The pouch felt heavy in her hands.

Just then, the morning bells rang. Julia hid away the pouch in her drawer where she kept her caps and kerchiefs. She and Blanche hurriedly dressed for breakfast. They were on their way to the servants' dining room when Sam stopped them and said, "Julia, Mr. Ames wishes to see you in his office right away."

Before Julia could stop herself, she burst out, "Oh, what now?" She threw a helpless glance at Blanche. "Will you come with me?"

"Certainly," said Blanche. Julia had the feeling Blanche was pleased by her request, but Sam said, "Mr. Ames wishes to see Julia alone."

"All right," Blanche said. She stood back and watched as Sam took Julia's elbow and steered her toward the front of the house.

They'd gone a short distance when Sam said, "Julia, is something wrong?"

"I don't know. I hope not."

"I've been wanting to speak to you. I know this isn't a good time–" he broke off nervously.

Julia felt she couldn't handle any more surprises. "Speak to me about what?"

"Nothing in particular. I just wanted to talk to you."

She glanced at him and found him watching her closely. She recognized the look on his face and knew what he wanted. She felt herself softening.

"My room is in the north wing," he said. "I have a small sitting room of my own. I hope sometime you will join me for tea."

"Maybe," she said, but she knew she would never join him for tea. Sometime soon, perhaps even tomorrow morning, in the dark hour before dawn, she would be gone from the house. Even if not, her life was already far too complicated.

He stopped walking and turned to face her. Reluctantly she stopped as well. For the first time, she looked closely at him. He was older than she'd supposed at first, probably at least thirty. He seemed to be a calm and staid sort of person.

Then he startled her by whispering, "I know what's happening."

Good Lord! Did everyone in this house know everything? "What is happening?" she asked.

"I know that Lord Guildford is pursuing you. And I know you don't want him."

She smiled at this. Sam had evidently drawn a different conclusion about her feelings than Blanche. It seemed to her that Sam was the better judge of character.

"What I wish to do," Sam said, "is pledge my friendship and assure you that if you need anything at all, I will serve you any way I can. If I can do anything to help you–"

"Thank you, Sam," she said, genuinely touched. How sweet he was, coming to her this way, so unlike the overbearing Lord Guildford, who simply assumed that all he had to do was crook his finger and she would fall into his bed.

"I can see that you are a girl of sterling character," he said. "I am surprised that Guildford thinks you could be a common mistress."

Common mistress. How embarrassing to have everyone speculating about her this way.

They started walking again and soon reached Mr. Ames' door. She glanced once at Sam, then knocked lightly. Mr. Ames called, "Enter." She opened the door and stepped inside.

"Come in and sit down," Mr. Ames said. He was sitting at a large mahogany desk pushed against the wall. The desk was cleared of everything except a single sheet of parchment. He turned his chair around to face her.

The room small, no more than three or four paces

across. It was windowless and warm, smelling faintly of lemon polish. She sat in the seat facing him.

"I warned you not to send letters on behalf of Lady Cecilia, but it has been reported to me that that the people to whom you sent your letters, Alice and John, have the same Christian names as a certain family named Brandon."

Anxiety tightened her chest. She said nothing.

"It may be a coincidence of names," he said, "or you may be helping Lady Cecilia send letters."

Before she could make up her mind how to respond, he said, "Are you aware of who John Brandon is?"

He must have taken her startled silence for a denial, because he said, "I will tell you. John Brandon was formerly the mayor of a town called Worthing. Because his son has been thrown into prison and then became involved with common thieves, he has lost his post as mayor. Do you understand the gravity of Lady Cecilia corresponding with such a family?"

Julia swallowed. He expected an answer, so said, "Yes, sir."

"Until you are cleared from suspicion, every letter you send from this house, from now on, must go through me."

She wondered how she might be cleared of suspicion. She supposed he was planning to inquire about John and Alice in Burgess Hill. It wouldn't be long before he learned the truth. She'd have to leave as soon as possible the following morning.

"I assume you understand the seriousness of this situation," he said.

"Yes, sir, I do."

He picked the piece of parchment off his desk and handed it to her. "You are to read and sign this document to indicate that you've been warned and you understand there may be serious consequences. I suspect, but I cannot prove, that my warning the first day did not stop you from disobeying me. If I had any more tangible evidence that you were smuggling Lady Cecilia's letters, I would dismiss you immediately. If you are caught aiding in forbidden correspondence, you will receive no references, and of course, be expected to return your advanced wages."

Advanced wages. Yes, of course. If she left her position or was dismissed, she would be expected to return the unearned wages.

He handed her a document and paused while she looked at it. "Do you understand this document?"

No, she didn't understand. There was Latinate and legalistic writing, and something about how smuggling letters would be considered the equivalent of corrupting Lady Cecilia.

Mr. Ames handed her a quill.

Her hand was trembling as she took the quill. She considered refusing to sign, but if she did that, she would be dismissed immediately, without the chance to get Cecilia's letters and the sack of coins Geoffrey needed.

She signed the warning and handed it back.

"Good," he said. "Now you may be excused. Remember that you have been warned."

Julia was late to the servant's dining room, arriving when the others had almost finished their meal. She ate quickly. Once, when she caught Blanche looking at her, she gave Blanche a quick earnest look which she hoped assured her that she would reveal everything as soon as possible.

After the meal, when she and Blanche were alone in the corridor, Blanche whispered, "What happened?"

"I'll tell you," Julia said, "but let's go back so I can tell Lady Cecilia as well."

Julia and Blanche arrived back in Lady Cecilia's rooms, but Lady Cecilia was still at breakfast with her family; as usual, the family lingered over their meals much longer than the servants.

"Tell me now," said Blanche. "I can't wait!"

So Julia told her about the order she'd been forced to sign, and that that she'd already raised suspicion by addressing her parents by their Christian names. Then she said, "Here's the worst, something I entirely forgot. The money I sent home to my parents is advance against my wages. If I leave and don't come back, or if am not allowed back, I will not be entitled to the money!"

"So?" asked Blanche.

"What do you mean, so? The money won't belong to me. How can I use it?"

"I cannot believe you are worried about that," Blanche said.

"But it isn't really my money."

"Julia. For heaven's sake. Lord Guildford and his uncles have caused your family's ruin!"

"But I'm not entitled to the money," she said. "And besides, to be fair, some of it was Geoffrey's fault."

"Are you for real?" Blanche asked.

Julia, startled, said, "What do you mean?"

"You are. I didn't believe it at first. I thought you were cunning and clever. I even wondered if you knew who Lady Cecilia was when you applied for the post. But I can see now you are genuinely and truly an innocent."

"Blanche, people accused of theft can end up in prison, or worse! Look at my brother!"

"If Lord Guildford believes you are deceiving him, he may want to slap your face. Or come to think of it, he may prefer to slap your bottom. But I rather doubt he's going to have you put into prison."

Julia felt a rush of embarrassment over the idea of Lord Guildford slapping her bottom.

Blanche took down her sewing basket and sat in the window seat to mend the lace on one of Lady Cecilia's sleeves. Julia went to the window and looked out. Two gardeners were at work trimming the hedges.

Idly, Julia asked, "Are you happy here?"

"This is easily the best post I've ever had. You can see we're practically lady companions to Cecilia. Some of that will change when the restrictions are lifted and she can have her friends visiting or when she marries and has more freedom, but I doubt I'll ever have to move back to the servant's quarters."

Lady Cecilia came back from breakfast, closed her door, and flopped down onto the bed. "They talk, they laugh, they linger over their meal, they make little jokes, as if everything is perfectly normal and my heart is not broken! They'll all find out soon enough that I'm determined to have my way!" She lowered her voice and said, "Once Geoffrey is free–" her voice trailed off.

Blanche put down her sewing and sat on the bed beside Cecilia.

"Julia has a concern."

Cecilia sat up. "What concern?"

"She says she cannot use her advance wages to free Geoffrey because she is not entitled to them."

"She's not entitled to them?" To Julia, Cecilia said, "What are you talking about?"

"They are advanced wages," Julia explained. "If I leave, or I am dismissed, I will be expected to return them."

Cecilia laughed outright at this. "I give you that money, Julia. Your advanced wages are a gift from me."

"I told her," said Blanche, "to think of the money as compensation for the harm done to her family."

"Exactly! My uncles and brother owe you that money for all you and your family has suffered at the hands of their pride!"

Julia didn't argue. What would be the point?

It was midmorning and Julia was in the garden just outside the kitchen clipping fresh gardenias for Lady Cecilia's dressing table. She imagined herself sneaking from the house in the early morning just before dawn. She'd felt so brave when she and Cecilia and Blanche first discussed the idea, but now, left to her thoughts, she felt fearful at the thought of creeping from the house with money not belonging to her.

The kitchen door opened and Sam came out. "I must speak to you," he said.

Her first thought was that he had come to warn her of fresh troubles. But one look at his earnest, bashful expression reassured her. She thought there was sadness in his eyes. She put the gardenias she'd clipped into her basket and stood up straight.

It occurred to her, standing there looking into Sam's face, that Sam had the same knowing gleam in his eye that Blanche had. He had the round, alert eyes of a man who watched carefully all that went on around him.

"What is it, Sam?"

"I have a note to give to you."

He handed her a folded note, sealed with Lord Guildford's own seal. She looked at Sam. "I wonder what it can be?" she said, more to herself than Sam.

"I don't know what the note says, but I can guess."

"You can?"

"I have been in service in this house for ten years, since Lord Guildford was eighteen years old. It is easy enough to guess the contents of this note. I know you do not wish to become his mistress, but I fear if I wait I will lose my chance. So please listen to what I have to say."

"Oh, Sam. Please, no–"

"Just listen! I will be leaving service soon to go into business with my brothers. I have two brothers, and we have been saving for years so that we could open a glove shop in Brighton. My oldest brother is an excellent tailor and I know our business will be a success. Julia, you would make me the happiest of men if you would consent–"

"Please stop!" she cried. She knew exactly where this was going. She also knew from her mother's training what she should say should a man propose marriage. She should say: I am not unaware of the honor you have bestowed on me by offering to make me your wife, but this is so sudden, I need time to give your offer the consideration it deserves.

Naturally, this hadn't been the speech she'd been planning to give Lord Guildford the morning he took her riding–but she didn't want to think about the things she had expected from Lord Guildford that morning. Now, she had Sam in front of her, looking at her imploringly, and she couldn't bear to disappoint him.

"Julia," he persisted, "can you love a man such as me?"

The directness of this question took her by surprise. She glanced toward the house, but nobody was in sight. "Please," she begged, "can we talk of this another time?" She didn't want to talk about this another time. She never wanted to talk about it again! But she didn't want to be cruel.

He considered her, then said, "Of course. I only hope you will refuse the request in Lord Guildford's note as well."

With that, he inclined his head, and turned and left. She opened the note and read:

Dearest Julia,
I wish to have a <u>discussion</u> with you. I desire to speak with you on an important philosophical and metaphysical question. The question I wish to discuss

is: What is love? As master of Guildford Manor, I command you to attend me in my parlor this evening after supper at seven o'clock so we can settle upon an answer to this question. I remain yours to command..

She folded the note and tucked it into her waistband, then picked up her basket and returned to Cecilia's chambers where she found Cecilia sitting in her window seat with a book. Julia took the note from the basket and handed it to Cecilia.

Cecilia unfolded the note and read it quickly. "What will you do? Will you go?"

"I don't know. What do you think?"

Blanche, who must have heard everything, came in from the adjoining parlor. She reached for the letter, read it, and laughed. "A metaphysical discussion, indeed!"

"Yes," said Julia. "He's mocking me."

"He's mocking you," said Blanche, "and he's planning to seduce you."

"I am not afraid of him, and no, Blanche, he cannot tempt me, not given the things I know about him now."

"But do you think you should go?" Cecilia asked.

"I think I must. He has commanded me. If I don't, he may come looking for me later tonight, or worse, in the morning, and it will be harder for you to hide my departure. I'll think of some ploy. I will promise to meet him again on my next day off. That way, he won't look for me again for a few days, and by then, I'll be all the way to London!"

"I think that will work," Cecilia said, "as long as you don't get your foot caught in the door."

"What my lady means," said Blanche, "is that will work, as long as you don't get your petticoat caught in his bed."

Lord Guildford was waiting in his private parlor at seven. He'd chosen their meeting place carefully. The room was private without being overly intimate. It had an air of formality with books lining the shelves and gilded portraits on the walls. The richly paneled walls were stately and elegant. At the same time, the room was inviting and warm, with deeply cushioned chairs, including two high wing-backed chairs facing the fireplace. It was his private parlor and attached to his private apartments, so nobody would enter without knocking, but it had a door to the main upstairs corridor, so it had the feel of a public room as well.

He was composed, and ready. When the soft knock came at the door, he said, "Enter."

Julia came in wearing her daytime apron and mob cap, with her hair primly tucked into her cap. He was displeased to see how she was dressed. He fully understood what she was doing, he just didn't understand why. She wished to emphasize that she was a servant in the house–but why she was doing this, he had no idea. The dress she wore beneath the apron was a simple servant's dress, the ribbons of the bodice laced tightly. Did she think he would find her less alluring in an apron? Or perhaps she thought the apron created a barrier of some sort?

"You wish to speak with me, my lord."

"I do indeed. Come in."

She stepped inside, but did not close the door behind her.

"Please sit down," he said, and gestured toward the settee. She glanced down at the richly upholstered and deeply cushioned settee, then stood up straighter. In her face was alarm.

He inclined his head graciously and gestured again toward the settee. "You may sit in my presence. I told you, Julia, when we are alone we can set aside all trappings of rank and distinction."

"Yes," she said so softly he could scarcely hear her. "We can set aside trappings of rank and distinction, when we are alone."

He understood her meaning. So she had come prepared to spar with him. Very well. If that was what she wanted, he would spar as well.

She remained standing. Was she hesitating because the settee was so deeply cushioned and luxurious? Did the upholstery, perhaps, remind her of a bed? He pulled a straight-backed chair from its position against the wall and said, "You may sit here, if you prefer."

"Thank you, my lord." She perched uneasily on the chair. He went to the door and closed it.

On the sideboard were two long-stemmed glasses and a bottle of white wine so rich the color had a golden tint. He uncorked the bottle and poured two glasses of wine. He didn't ask her if she wanted wine because he knew she'd say no. He simply poured two glasses and handed one to her. She held her glass awkwardly for a moment, then reached to put it on a nearby table.

Her features were carefully composed, but hands

71

trembled slightly. If not for the slight trembling of her hands when she set down the wine glass, he would have detected no emotion in her at all. On the table was a white porcelain dish filled with coins. His solicitor had brought them, and he'd carelessly left them out. He saw her gaze rest briefly on the coins, then she turned quickly away. The coins seemed to fluster her slightly. How careless of him to have left out so crude a symbol of commerce.

He moved so he was standing very close to her, close enough so he could easily brush against her—but he carefully kept from touching her. His closeness had the effect he intended. She tensed slightly, expecting him to make a move toward her.

Instead he calmly sipped his wine and said, "Heavenly. Perfect. You really should try it, Julia."

"Thank you, my lord, I will." She made no move to take the wine.

He set his glass down. Then he pulled a chair for himself from its position against the wall and set it down near enough to hers so he could touch her should he choose to, but not so close that he would upset her calm. He didn't want to upset her calm—at least not yet.

"What shall we talk about first?" he asked.

"I don't know, my lord."

"I think we should talk about you. Who you are. Where you are from."

Her eyes widened slightly. "I would rather not talk about me, my lord."

"But, Julia," he kept his voice soft and low, "I truly want to know more about you. I want to discover whether you are a girl I can love."

"I do not believe I am a girl you can love."

"I am the only person who can properly answer that question. And before I can do so, I must learn all about you."

"Really, my lord, I would rather not talk about myself now."

He sat back, considering her. Her hands were folded in her lap. From this vantage point he could see the sweet curve of her breast which showed plainly even under a simple muslin servant's dress. Her waist was so tiny he believed he could entirely encircle her waist with his hands. He felt his heartbeat quickening.

"But you were willing to talk about yourself the morning we went riding," he said. "Is that not correct?"

She took a deep breath, as if weighing what to tell him. She then surprised him by reaching for her wine glass and taking a sip. He knew from the way she sipped, tasted the wine, and sipped again that she was accustomed to fine wine. He said, "You are drinking a sauterne from Sauternais region of the Graves section in Bordeaux."

"Yes, my lord," she said, as if entirely familiar with sauterne.

Now, what did a lady's maid know of sauterne? It occurred to him that she wasn't a lady's maid at all, but was some sort of imposter in his house. She'd read Herrick. She obviously had an education superior to the average lady's maid. With the exception of wearing her apron this evening and hesitating to sit in his presence, she behaved as if she were a duchess.

Yes, she was acting like a duchess, and he was treating her like one. Once Guildford got past the absurd notion that he was wooing a girl wearing a mob cap and apron in exactly the same way and using the same tone of voice he might woo a duchess, he entered the game with enthusiasm, going back to his unanswered question. "You were willing to talk about yourself the day we went riding, but not now?

"Yes, my lord."

"Why then, but not today?"

"I cannot tell you."

What on earth? "Julia, are you toying with me?"

"No, my lord. There is something–" she faltered. "Something I cannot tell you now." She looked directly at him with a look so sad and earnest he melted.

"When will you be able to tell me?"

"Perhaps–" she looked away. Without looking back at him, she said, "May I tell you Tuesday?"

"*Tuesday?*"

"Yes, my lord. My next day off."

He felt a laughter coming into his chest. This conversation was feeling faintly ridiculous. "Perhaps, Julia, you only reveal personal secrets on Tuesdays?"

This caused a ripple of emotion to flow through her, like a shudder he could see plainly. He watched, hoping that she would smile, but even in profile, he could see her expression remained somber. Her face was turned away just far enough so he couldn't even see if there was a glint of amusement in her eyes.

"I am joking with you, Julia."

She still didn't smile.

He hadn't intended to touch her–not yet, anyway–but he touched her chin and turned her face toward him. He saw in her eyes why she did not smile. She was frightened. Deeply frightened.

"All right then," he said. "For now, we will talk about something else." He took a drink of wine. "I think perhaps we should talk about love. I asked you an important question the day we went riding. I don't believe you answered, so I will ask again. How would you define love, Julia?"

"I–" she faltered.

He couldn't help smiling. It wasn't a fair question, of course. Her eyes were now bright and glassy, her lips and cheeks deeply flushed. The color in her face reminded him of how easily he was able to arouse her. Sitting this close to her was maddening. His entire body felt tense and alive. How easy it would be right now, to pull her toward him. He had no doubt she would resist, at first, but remembering how readily she'd responded to him in the past, he fully believed he could overcome her resistance, quite easily. However, he did not want to move too quickly and send her fleeing from the house. His plan was to proceed more slowly this time, so he could maneuver her into the long-term situation he desired.

"I would like for you to feel something." He took her hand very gently and pressed her open palm to his heart, which he knew was thumping hard enough for her to feel this pulse.

She remained perfectly still. "Your heart, too, is beating quickly–is it not?"

She looked down into her lap.

"Please look at me," he whispered. She tipped her face up so that she was looking into his eyes. Her eyes were thickly lashed, the bristling of her lashes setting off the deep blue of her eyes. Yes, her eyes were nothing short of magnificent.

"This feeling," he said, "the way I feel right now with my heart beating fast. Is this not love?"

He did not expect her to answer. He was therefore completely startled when she said, very quietly, "No, my lord, it is not."

No, my lord, it is not? She flat-out contradicted him?

He stood up and went to the bookcase and pulled out a volume of Shakespeare. He flipped to the passage he was looking for, and read:

"What is love, tis not hereafter
Present mirth hath present laughter
What's to come is still unsure.
In delay there lies no plenty.
Then come kiss me, sweet and twenty,
Youth's a stuff will not endure."

He finished reading and closed the book and returned it to the shelf. He went back to his chair.

"You disagree with the poet's viewpoint, I take it?"

"Yes, my lord, I disagree."

"You think the poet was wrong?"

"Yes. I believe poets are often wrong. Shakespeare writes beautifully, but there are certain things he may not understand."

So she recognized the passage as one of Shakespeare's. "And you," he said, "a maid of perhaps one and twenty years, are an expert in matters of passion?"

"You asked for my opinion, my lord. Even a

lady's maid of–" she hesitated a moment, and said, "not much more than twenty years may have an opinion."

Now he was astonished. For all that this girl seemed the very picture of sweetness and vulnerability, she also had the courage to quietly defy him.

"What really intrigues me," he said, "and what I most wonder about is how you came to be so familiar with Shakespeare and Herrick."

She looked at him, alarmed. Perhaps she was remembering that lady's maids are not supposed to have read Shakespeare. If she was an imposter, a well-bred girl masquerading as a lady's maid, she was a very clumsy one, carelessly revealing her familiarity with the literature of past centuries.

"Tell me why you disagree," he said. "Is love indeed to be found in an afterlife, perhaps, or, as the poet claims, is love to be found now, when the blood runs warm and life quickens the pulse?"

"I disagree because the rules that apply to men are different from the rules that apply to girls. It is easy enough for a man to indulge in the pleasures of the moment, but for a girl to do the same–" she looked away and colored visibly.

So she was a girl of practicalities, as well as a romantic. "Here is a pleasure of the moment which I believe you can safely indulge in." He stood up and walked to a table bearing a lamp and a candy dish. The dish contained fine chocolates from Italy. He brought the dish back to her and sat down.

"You have read Shakespeare and Herrick. You have tasted fine wine from Bordeaux. Do you know what these are?"

She looked at the chocolates in the dish and said, "No, my lord. I do not."

"They are chocolates. Have you ever tasted chocolate?"

"I have had chocolate to drink, my lord."

"This is something new, chocolate you can bite." He picked up one of the chocolates and offered it to her.

"No, my lord!" The fright was back in her face.

"What a little Puritan you are! You must taste this chocolate, Julia."

"I would rather not, please!"

He was amazed to see she was genuinely alarmed. "Do you think I have put something in this chocolate, a potion perhaps that will cause you to swoon in my arms? Is that your fear?"

Something like amusement came into her eyes. So she could respond to humor. This time he thought perhaps she would smile, but she still didn't. She remained entirely alert and watchful, like an animal being hunted.

"Watch," he said. "I will eat half of it." He took a bite of the chocolate, smiled, and said, "Mmm," allowing his face to show deep delight. Then he offered her the other half. "Go ahead," he said. "It is safe. And delicious."

She took the chocolate, considered it for a moment, and put it in her mouth.

"Hold it on your tongue," he said. "Let it rest there. Let it melt."

He watched her face, gratified by what he saw. First, she was startled. How could she not be startled by the novel sensation of velvety chocolate melting in her mouth? Slowly, despite herself, a look of

78

reluctant pleasure spread over her features.

"What do you think of Venetian chocolate, Julia."

Naturally, with a mouth full of melting chocolate, it took a moment before she could respond. "It is very good, my lord."

"It is, indeed. The pity is that we have so short a time on earth to enjoy such things as fine chocolates."

The effect of the chocolate was not long lasting. Soon her face returned to its former carefully composed expression. Standing this close, he saw the great effort required to keep her face so impassive. He marveled at her control.

"Ah, Julia," he adopted the tone he might use if musing to himself. "We never know what tomorrow will bring. But we are here, now. We can enjoy this room, this wine, this chocolate, the cushions on these chairs."

"You would have me use these things as if they belong to me?"

"These things do not belong to me, either. If you want to stand on points, this house and everything in it belongs to the earl. But really, in a manner of speaking, he doesn't own them either. Life, and everything we touch, is only ours to borrow. One day our youth will be spent, and in time we will be gone completely, and others will be enjoying all that we failed to enjoy. That, my lovely Julia, is why the poets admonish us to seize the moment."

She was watching him closely, an intelligent gleam in her eyes. He wondered what she was thinking, but he knew she would not tell. So he said, "Now, Julia, here is what I really want to know. How is it that a lady's maid is familiar with Shakespeare, familiar with Herrick, and has tasted wine from

Bordeaux?"

Various emotions flitted across her features. He suspected she was trying to decide what she should tell him. He kept his voice quiet to soften the command and said, "Julia, you must tell me what you are withholding."

"Tuesday," she whispered. "I will tell you my secret on Tuesday."

"Oh, yes, I forgot. We must wait for the day designated for revealing secrets. Shall we go riding again on Tuesday?"

She hesitated, but for only a moment. "Yes," she said quietly.

Now he knew she was playing some sort of game with him. Given what had happened last time they'd gone riding, and given how primly she sat now in his parlor, it simply did not make sense that she would agree so readily to go riding with him again. Something was off, and he had no intention of waiting until Tuesday to find out what it was.

"Before I agree to wait until Tuesday to learn this secret, you must give me one good reason, one really good reason, why you cannot tell me now."

She looked at him, considering. Her lower lip trembled. For a dreadful moment, he believed she would cry. When she spoke, her whisper was so quiet he had to strain to hear. "Because I believe when you learn my secret you will cast me from the house."

He wondered if she was dramatizing. His highly emotional sister Cecilia frequently overreacted, throwing herself into hysterics far beyond what was called for in a particular situation.

"It is that bad?" he asked.

"Yes."

He stood up and paced, walking first to the bookshelf and lightly touching the spine of a book, then back to the table where he had set his glass of wine. He drank some wine, then looked at her. He supposed she had done something of which she was ashamed, perhaps something serious enough to have caused her to fall from society's graces. It occurred to him that she wasn't as virginal as she pretended. She could, perhaps, be that good an actress. He was prepared to forgive her, whatever she had done.

"All right, Julia. We will go riding on Tuesday. Now you may leave, if you wish."

He could see she was surprised by this.

They stood up together and he walked with her to the door. Before opening the door, he turned to her. He bowed formally, feeling faintly ridiculous to be bowing to a girl wearing a serving apron and mob cap, but if this was how she wanted it, he would go along. He would court her as if she were a duchess.

He reached for her hand and kissed it. He knew then from warmth that poured from her and the deep color in her cheeks that he could easily tempt her back into his arms. He needed only to reach for her, and she would come to him.

But he would wait. He put his hand on the doorknob.

The sudden way she looked at him made him know she had something to say. "What is it, Julia?"

"You say you feel tenderness for me?"

"Indeed, I do," he said.

"On the road you sought to protect me from your friends."

"I will always seek to protect you." He heard the

glib tone of his own voice, and didn't like it.

"Then I have one request I beg of you." She turned her face up to him. She seemed so vulnerable and heartbreakingly young, he thought she couldn't possibly be deceiving him about anything. What could be hidden behind so sweet a face?

"Ask anything, my lovely Julia."

"When you learn my secret, and you may learn it before Tuesday, will you please recall the tenderness you feel for me at this moment, and try to retain at least some of it?"

That was easy to promise because really, she wasn't asking much. "I promise," he said.

Just then, came the scraping of a chair near the fireplace. Guildford, startled beyond words, felt his heart skip a beat. Julia was so startled she gave a small gasp. Indeed, one of the wingback chairs facing the fireplace moved. Next came a small cough. Then the earl, Guildford's great-uncle, emerged from the chair. He appeared to have been asleep. He stood up shakily, his body so bent and rickety, looked as though he would fall to the ground like a heap of bones.

"Uncle!" Guildford cried. "Let me help you!" Guildford flew to his side and took his arm.

"Ring for Mr. Ames," the earl said, his voice raspy and trembly.

"Certainly," Guildford said. He helped the earl to the door, and rang the bell for the butler.

The earl then faced Guildford and, in a raspy but understandable voice, said, "Stop tormenting that poor girl."

Tormenting? Guildford looked at Julia, who was as shocked as he was.

82

Guildford said, "Of course, uncle." To Julia, he said, "You may go, of course."

She bobbed a quick curtsey, picked up her skirts and was about to run off when the old earl held out a hand to stop her. "A moment," he said, his voice aquiver. She kept her chin down, but ventured a glance up at the old earl, who reached for her hand, and kissed the back of her hand as if she were indeed a duchess.

Now for the first time since entering his parlor, Julia actually smiled and her face came alive. She curtseyed again, evidently enjoying the moment, flashing another brilliant smile. What Guildford felt just then was intense envy that she should smile so joyfully at his elderly uncle but show him nothing but caution and fear.

She backed away. When she was almost out of sight, she picked up her skirts, turned, and hurried away.

Guildford turned to his great-uncle as if expecting to find an apparition instead of a living, breathing human being.

"I love you dearly," the old man said slowly, each of his words requiring great effort, "like a son."

Guildford started to speak, but the earl held up a hand to silence him.

"But that girl," he said, poking Guildford's chest with a bony and bent finger, "has a rare spirit."

Just then Mr. Ames appeared from around the corner. Seeing Guildford and the earl together, he stopped and bowed from the waist.

"Help me to my rooms," the old man said. His next words came out slowly and with great effort: "Let us leave this young man to his conscience."

"Certainly, your lordship," said Mr. Ames, offering an arm to the earl. Guildford watched them walk slowly from his parlor. When they turned the corner toward the earl's private apartments, he closed the door. For a moment he stood just inside the door, still amazed. Then he went to sit in the same chair the earl had been sitting in, facing the fireplace, its back to the room.

Guildford sat quietly for a long time in that chair, which was warm and smelled faintly of the earl's tobacco and mints.

Julia walked from Lord Guildford's parlor up the main staircase directly to Lady Cecilia's chambers, stunned by what had just occurred, and feeling so relieved she was ready to collapse with nervous exhaustion. Who would have expected the old earl to rise from the depths of a winged-back chair and chastise Lord Guildford that way? Had he been sleeping in that chair? Or had he been listening to all?

And to think he'd accused Guildford of tormenting her!

It had been a battle of wills, but he'd evidently been enjoying the battle–up until the moment the earl rose from that chair. Now that she knew the earl had been in the room the entire time, all she could do was utter a prayer of thanks that she had so carefully controlled herself at all times, never for a moment letting down her guard. Suppose, just suppose, she had lost control right there in the parlor the way she had when she and Lord Guildford had gone riding. The thought of the old earl witnessing such a scene brought such a rush of embarrassment that her knees felt weak.

Still, all things considered, even with the delicious surprise at the end, the meeting had not gone well. Lord Guildford had managed to fluster her. He guessed too much. She hadn't expected him to watch her so closely, to pry so cleverly into her thoughts, to try so hard to discern precisely who she was. Like Blanche, she'd expected him to try harder to assault her senses and wear down her defenses so that she would surrender her body to him.

Outside the door to Cecilia's chambers, she paused to compose herself. She entered the side room she shared with Blanche, and found it empty. She knocked softly on Lady Cecilia's door.

"Enter!" said Cecilia.

Julia entered. Blanche and Cecilia were sitting on the bed in their chemises, cross-legged, like very young girls. She went to sit beside them.

"You're back sooner than I expected," said Blanche. "What happened?"

Julia looked at Blanche, whose face showed intense curiosity but no envy. Well, why should she feel envious now? By morning Julia would be gone from the house probably forever, most likely cast as a villain like her brother.

"Well?" Blanche asked impatiently. "What did he do? Tell us?"

Remembering, Julia giggled. "He gave me wine and chocolate, and we talked about the meaning of love."

"And then he just let you leave?" Cecilia asked.

"I promised I would go riding with him on Tuesday. He knows there is something I am hiding."

"That doesn't surprise me," said Cecilia. "My brother is smart, particularly when consumed with a purpose. However, my grand and noble brother, the epicure and seducer of women, may find himself bested in the next few days."

"Something else happened in his parlor," Julia said. "Something most surprising."

"What!" Cecilia and Blanche cried in unison.

"The entire time I was there, the earl was in a high backed chair, hidden from view. He revealed himself at the end, chastised Lord Guildford for tormenting me, then kissed my hand as if I were a great lady."

"Really," said Cecilia. She was quiet for a moment, then said, "I always wonder how much he understands of what is happening. People say in his day he was considered the most honorable and well-mannered of noblemen."

"He still is, if you ask me. Lord Guildford could use some lessons from him."

"Well," said Blanche. "We'd better get you ready."

Julia went into the room she shared with Blanche and packed her few possessions into her knapsack–a few extra caps and kerchiefs and undergarments, her toothcloth.

"Take these with you, too," Cecilia said, bringing a small diamond brooch and a dress she'd rolled into a tight bundle. "If you can pass in London as a lady of rank, people will be less likely to trouble you."

"Yes, I agree. Thank you." She rolled the dress and brooch into her knapsack.

Cecilia went to her writing desk, and with help

from both Julia and Blanche, drafted the letter Geoffrey needed. She wrote two copies, one for Julia to put into her knapsack and another for her waistband. Better to have two, she said, just in case. She also wrote a letter saying that Julia Brandon was going forth from Guildford Manor under the direction of Lady Cecilia and with instructions to carry out her business, bearing gifts given to her by Lady Cecilia herself. Cecilia sealed this with her own seal as well. "To protect you," Cecilia explained. "In case you get caught."

Julia put this letter in the knapsack. She didn't believe the letter would help her much, though, should she get caught.

"The problem is," said Cecilia, "I'm afraid we haven't enough money. Geoffrey may need more than we have, and you'll have to hire a coach to take you to London. We need to figure out how to get more money."

"There's a dish of gold coins," Julia said, "in your brother's private parlor. I saw it there."

"A dish of gold coins?" Cecilia said. She and Blanche looked at each other. To Julia, Cecilia said, "Are you sure?"

"Quite sure, yes."

"I suppose it is like my brother to leave large amounts of money laying around. When the household has gone to sleep, I will go to his parlor and see if they are still there."

In the next moment, Julia regretted mentioning the coins. At the same time, she knew she needed whatever money she could lay her hands on. "But if you take the coins, he will know right away that they are missing! There will be a search and they will discover that I am gone."

"The only solution I can see," said Cecilia, "is for you to leave tonight. That way, you'll be home before dawn, and you'll be on your way to London before my brother can possibly find the coins missing."

She felt a rush of apprehension at the idea of taking Guildford's gold, which she knew raised the stakes considerably. It was one thing to leave with five pounds belonging to Cecilia. It was another to leave with much more belonging to Lord Guildford. But what could she do? Risk getting all the way to London without the money she needed?

"Is there a moon tonight?" Julia asked, going to the window.

Blanche joined her at the window and said, "I believe there is." Suddenly, Blanche said, "Why doesn't Julia just take a horse!"

"Certainly," said Julia. "Why not? As long as Lord Guildford and his uncles will have criminal charges to bring against me, why not also hang me as a horse thief?"

"Nobody is going to hang you as a horse thief, Julia," said Cecilia. "Blanche is right. Take a horse. No, let me phrase that better. I will lend you a horse from our stables. In fact, I will lend you one of my own. Now we just need to wait until the house is quiet so I can steal my brother's coins."

Cecilia settled herself back against the pillows of her bed and said, "Julia, tell me about Geoffrey!"

"What do you want to know?"

"What was he like before I knew him? What was he like as a child?"

Julia sat on the stool not far from Cecilia. "He's eight years older than me. Three children were born between us, and all three died, so I was the petted and spoiled baby. Nobody petted and spoiled me more than Geoffrey. He never returned from town without gifts for me. I adored him."

"This does not surprise me," said Cecilia. "I knew the moment I met him that he had a kind and generous disposition."

Julia thought about the side of her brother she had no intention of sharing with Cecilia, his wild, reckless side, though Cecilia probably already knew something about that. Cecilia was not the first girl to have fallen in love with Geoffrey. Many of the girls of Worthing had also loved him, often being kind to Julia in the hopes that she'd put in a good word with her brother. Geoffrey was a good, strong rider, but exasperated their mother by jumping the highest of fences. He was a good gambler, and nearly always won, but he drove their father to distraction by the high stakes for which he would play. Julia had seen many of the neighborhood girls' disappointment when Geoffrey didn't give them the love and attention they had hoped for. The meanest of Worthing's gossips had said it was no wonder such a wild young man ended up in prison.

"He's also a bit headstrong," Julia said.

"I know that, too," said Cecilia. "I remembered how he behaved when Robert had him pinned to the ground. If Geoffrey had just given in, if he had only promised to stay away from me, he would not be in prison now. But he would not promise." There was evident pride in her voice.

"My parents would say he is foolish as well as headstrong," said Julia.

"I imagine they are furious with him," said

Cecilia.

"They are." She was tempted to tell Cecilia that her parents were angry at her as well. She wondered what Cecilia would say if she told her about her mother's plan for sending her to London. Cecilia, who had loathed the idea of marrying a man like Sir Ruthven, would probably sympathize with her. Blanche, however, would never understand.

"Our brothers have much in common," Cecilia said quietly, "but in other ways, they are so different. Robert is, on the surface, all fun and gallantry. His philosophy of living seems to be if one is good, two are better. If dancing is pleasurable, let us dance all night. He has a good heart, and truly wants others to enjoy life. The problem is that he lives too much in the moment. Sometimes he doesn't like to look too deeply into matters or think too precisely about what he is doing or how people around him are really feeling."

"What will he do when he finds that I am missing?"

"I honestly don't know," said Cecilia. "Lately he has been surprising me."

"Do you think he'll call the constable and send the authorities after me if he figures out I took money and a horse?"

"I don't believe so," said Cecilia. "My uncles might want to, and that horrible butler certainly would want to, but my brother is enough of a gentleman to just let you go."

"He will let you go," said Blanche. "I don't believe he'd ever turn you over to the authorities as a thief. Lady Cecilia is too angry at him to agree, but he's as much a gentleman as the earl. I'm just hoping he'll look my way when this is all done and Julia is back with her family. I won't turn down his offers, I assure you."

Julia looked at Blanche, and a memory stirred. "Sam Mason is thinking about leaving service to open a glove shop with his brothers," she said.

"How do you know that?" asked Blanche.

Julia felt embarrassed remembering the things Sam had said to her. "He told me."

"You always dreamed of a shop of your own," Cecilia said to Blanche. "You certainly deserve a reward for all you have done for me."

Those were brave words, Julia knew, and kind words. Lady Cecilia, however, was hardly in a position to do much for anyone, given the trouble she was in now, and the worse trouble she was likely to be in later, should she succeed in her plan for getting Geoffrey out of prison.

When the house was finally quiet, and all the candles had been blown out, and the only lights remaining were a few torches here and there, Cecilia crept alone from the room in her slippers. Blanche and Julia waited nervously, listened to the ticking of the clock. She returned seven minutes later. It felt like an eternity.

She was flushed and happy. "I got the coins. It is a fortune. Fifty pounds. You will be able to hire a coach, Julia, and give Geoffrey the money he needs."

"Fifty pounds!" Julia cried. "I can't possibly take that much! That is more than we could possibly need."

"Take it all," said Cecilia. "You can return what you don't use. The important thing is for you to be safe and for Geoffrey to get out of prison."

"But fifty pounds!"

"Come on," Cecilia said. "If you had asked for it, you know my brother would have just handed you the money."

Blanche said, "Certainly he would have! Of course, he would have expected a form of gratitude Julia may not be prepared to give him." She laughed at Julia and said, "Just stop worrying!"

Being told to stop worrying had the opposite effect on Julia. She suddenly had a premonition that this might not go well. Cecilia, who was highly emotional, also seemed every bit as rash and impulsive as Geoffrey. Julia was filled with doubt, afraid things were getting out of hand.

Just after midnight, the moon was high enough in the sky so that Julia would be able to see her way home along the road. "I will go downstairs with you," Cecilia said, "to get a horse for you, and walk you to the road. If you get caught leaving, I want us caught together."

So together they slipped from Cecilia's room into the main corridor. Quietly, stealthily, they walked down the corridor to a narrow doorway leading to the servants' back stairs. They tiptoed down the stairs, then along the corridor leading to the deserted and darkened kitchens. They groped their way in the darkness.

Through the kitchens was a side door leading to the vegetable garden. What a relief it was to step outside into the fresh, crisp air with the starry night sky arching overhead. The air outside was still and warm, the leaves high in the trees rustling in the slightest breeze. Once outside, they crept along to the back of the house to the stables.

"I will give you my gray mare, Morning Star," whispered Cecilia. "She's gentle and will let anyone ride her."

Julia stood back while Cecilia took her mare and a saddle from the stables. When the horse was ready, they walked toward the road, keeping in the shadows near the groves out of sight of the windows. The moon was just high enough and just full enough to give the light they needed to avoid stumbling on rocks, or stepping into potholes in the road. Soon they reached the end of the avenue lined with firs and passed through the main gates of Guildford Manor.

Cecilia turned to Julia and gave her a warm hug. "Please keep safe."

Julia returned the hug, then mounted Morning Star and set off at a walk. The road, lined with hawthorn and mulberry hedges, dipped down into a gully divided by a narrow spring. She crossed the creek on a bridge of loose stones. Because of the darkness, she allowed the horse to walk as slowly as she wished. She rode as close to the hedges as she could, feeling better hidden. Overhead high among the branches, a bat flapped its wings.

The road was not familiar to her. She'd only been this way three times, always during broad daylight. She feared she would lose her way. The plan required that she make it home during the night so she could set out for London early in the morning, before anyone learned she had gone, and certainly before Guildford discovered his gold missing. She would have to be doubly careful not to take a wrong turn.

Because of her slow pace, it took more than an hour before she reached the deep bend in the road, which led to the crossroad. At the crossroad, she easily oriented herself, and knew immediately which road would take her to Burgess Hill.

When at last she reached the outskirts of Burgess Hill, the dew had grown heavy and her hands felt damp. Burgess Hill was considerably smaller than Worthing, consisting of a white-washed church in the middle of the town, surrounded by a half dozen streets lined with small shops. Thatched cottages, the eaves covered with lichen and moss, were set back some distance from the road. During the day the thatch was a covered moss, but in the moonlight, all the cottages appeared silvery-gray. Many had dormer windows wreathed in honeysuckle and ivy.

She recognized a familiar dip the road which, when she and her parents had first come to Burgess Hill, had been filled with water making the road difficult to travel. Just beyond the dip, lay the cottage her parents had rented, a row of white birches in front. She felt a sudden eagerness to see her parents again. The shutters were all pulled closed, as if her parents were in mourning.

She dismounted and tied the mare to a post, then tried the door and found it locked. She knocked as hard as she could. She heard nothing, so she knocked again. Soon she heard their hound, Ginger, give a series of short, quick barks. Then there was a rustling inside, and she saw in the window that someone had a candle. The door opened and Julia's mother rushed toward her. Ginger sniffed her legs, and licked her hand.

"Dear Lord, child," her mother said. "What are you doing here at this hour?"

Julia accepted her mother's embrace. "Oh, Mama! I have much to tell you."

"Come in!" Then her mother held her at arm's length and studied her. "Are you all right? Are you hurt?"

"I am fine, just very tired. And I have news that will amaze you."

"Come to the bedroom."

The cottage had a front parlor, a single bedroom, and a second room off the pantry which Julia had used as her bedroom. The house seemed smaller than she remembered it, smelling faintly of mold and dust.

Her father was sitting up in a chair which he evidently also used as a bed. She saw from his face how much he hated being confined.

"I am so sorry your back isn't better yet, Papa." She went to kiss his cheek.

"The doctor says it is worse because I tried to do too much too soon. He promised if I hold myself still for a few weeks I will be able to walk again."

Mr. Brandon had always been a man of great vitality, so it was unsettling to see him looking so fragile. She pulled up a stool to sit near him. Her mother sat on the bed.

"Talk!" her mother said. "Tell us what has happened. What are you doing here in the middle of the night?"

"I hardly know where to begin. First, I guess you

should know that Lady Cecilia Guildford is the girl who Geoffrey dueled over–"

"Geoffrey dueled over a lady?" said Mr. Brandon. "I assumed it was another gambling quarrel!"

"No, not a gambling quarrel." She explained how the uncle had challenged Geoffrey to a duel but Lord Guildford had fought him instead, how Geoffrey needed only promise to stay away from Lady Cecilia and the family would have released him.

When she finished, Mr. Brandon said, "I didn't whip that boy often enough."

Julia gave him a sharp look. "Papa, you know you never whipped him at all! You've never whipped anyone."

"Well, then, I should have," he said. "Often. Of all the foolish capers."

"They are accusing him of abducting Lady Cecilia by force. Lady Cecilia said all he had to do was promise to stay away from her and the family would have left him alone. But he would not promise."

"We have suffered all of this because of Geoffrey's pride?" Mrs. Brandon cried. "I should have whipped him as well!"

"Maybe he loves her," Julia said quietly.

"There you go again about love," said Mrs. Brandon. "This is a fine example, Julia, of where your idea of love can lead people." She sniffed and said, "I would call his behavior foolishness and pride, not love."

"What do you call it, Papa?" she asked.

"I call it reckless passion."

Julia did not argue. She believed Geoffrey's steadfastness and Cecilia's loyalty were indeed love. To Lord Guildford, she wanted to say: No, my lord–

love is not present mirth making present laughter. It is a steadfastness of purpose, a deep unwavering loyalty.

"You still haven't explained what you are doing here," Mrs. Brandon said. "Did you run away when you learned the truth about the Guildford family?"

"Not quite. Geoffrey sent a letter to Cecilia saying a barrister would lay his appeal before the magistrate, but he needed a letter from her swearing he never abducted her, and he needs money to pay the barrister. I brought the letter, and money." She opened her knapsack and showed her parents the gold she had brought. She removed the letters and handed them to her father.

"Julia!" her mother cried, "Look at this gold! This is a fortune!"

"Fifty-five pounds, to be exact."

"Fifty-five pounds!" her mother gasped.

"Five belonged to Lady Cecilia. Fifty we took from Lord Guildford's private parlor. He left them out in plain sight."

"Oh, dear Lord." Mrs. Brandon put her fingers to her temples and sat on the bed. She looked as if she was ready to swoon. "This money was stolen from Lord Guildford? Oh, Julia–"

Julia felt silly when she said, "I wasn't the one who took it from his parlor. Cecilia took it from his parlor."

"You took it from the house! That's worse!"

Meanwhile, Mr. Brandon unfolded the letters and began reading. When he spoke, his voice was measured and quiet, a startling juxtaposition to Mrs. Brandon's horror. "These letters may well get Geoffrey out of prison. When I was mayor, I would never have allowed a man to be arrested for abduction if the lady insisted she had gone willingly, no matter how angry the family was."

"We must bring Lady Cecilia's letters to Geoffrey," Julia said.

"Yes," Mr. Brandon said. "Geoffrey will see that the gold gets returned. I consider this his debt. Meanwhile, if he is innocent, and we have proof, we must show the constable."

"And we have to hurry," said Julia, "before someone realizes I've gone."

Mrs. Brandon was breathing heavily and again Julia afraid she would swoon. Her mother, a woman of practicalities was not the type to faint, but then, she'd just been told her daughter had left Guildford Manor with a horse and fifty pounds not belonging to her.

"First thing in the morning," said Mrs. Brandon, "I will go into town and hire a coach to take me to London. I don't like this, though, Julia. It's all very frightening. That is a powerful family."

"I think Julia should go with you to London," said Mr. Brandon.

"Why?" asked his wife.

"I feel fairly certain someone from Guildford Manor will call the authorities. They obviously want Geoffrey out of the way for a while, and will move quickly to prevent his release. I think it best for Julia not to be here if someone comes to question her. I will answer the questions."

"If the constable comes," Julia asked, "will you show him the letter Cecilia wrote giving me permission to take these things from the house?"

"If the constable comes, I will say as little as

possible, until Geoffrey is able to lay his claim before the magistrate."

"Why not hide Julia with a neighbor?" Mrs. Brandon asked.

"I am afraid if the constable becomes involved, and she remains here, they will find her quickly. You can hide her better at an inn in London while you go to the prison to see Geoffrey."

"But who will stay with you, Papa? You cannot get out of the chair, so you cannot be left alone!"

"Our neighbors will check in on your father while we are gone," Mrs. Brandon said. "Meanwhile, Julia must get a little sleep. We have much to do at daybreak, and the sun will rise in just a few hours."

She led her daughter to her bedroom off the pantry, helped her from her dress and into a nightshift, and tucked her into bed. She then left, taking the candle with her.

Julia found the smell of the room unfamiliar and unpleasant, particularly in the darkness. The room smelled of dust and something acrid Julia didn't recognize. She was so tired, though, the moment her head was on the pillow she easily gave into her exhaustion and fell into a deep, dreamless sleep.

Julia awakened to the smell of eggs frying. She opened her eyes, feeling that she hadn't slept at all. She went to the window. The sky was still dark, but she knew from the brightness in the east that the sun would soon rise.

Today, for her trip to London, she would wear the

dress Cecilia had given her, a fine dress that shimmered like silk. The dress made her think of Lord Guildford because the sleeves were the exact color of the sapphire he had offered her. The front was cut low, set with fine lace, and tied with a large flouncy bow. She pinned on the brooch Cecilia had lent her.

Suddenly Julia was aware of the irony of the situation. She hadn't wanted to go to London dressed in borrowed clothes and jewels, and here she was, going to London dressed in borrowed clothes and jewels. She hadn't wanted to deceive a future husband, but here she was, engaging in the behavior of common thief, creeping away from a great manor house with stolen money–and there was no denying that the fifty pounds had been stolen from Lord Guildford. No doubt, if this plan went awry, her family would be much worse off than before.

She was buttoning her shoes when she heard her mother call out, "Julia, come eat with us." All three ate together in her parents' bedroom, her father in his chair, Julia and her mother perched on the bed.

Her mother was already dressed in the finest dress she had brought with her from Worthing, a stripped silk taffeta of a rich golden color with a squared neckline set with lace, the sleeves reaching to her elbows. She smoothed her skirt and said, "Julia was right. Or, rather, Lady Cecilia was right. We must go dressed as ladies."

As Julia ate, she listened for the sounds of horses outside, afraid the constable was indeed coming to arrest her. "The sooner we are on our way to London," Julia said, "the better I will feel."

"The sooner this whole thing is over," said Mrs.

Brandon, "the better I will feel."

When the sun was just over the horizon and the shops in town would soon be opening, Mrs. Brandon put on her hat and left the house. Meanwhile, Julia packed for their trip. Packing didn't take much time. Mostly she needed to reassemble the things she had brought with her from Guildford House. In the front room which served as the only common family area, was a low book shelf filled with books. There were some Defoe novels, volumes of philosophy, legal treatises, plays, and poetry. Imagining long hours by herself in an inn while her mother went to the prison, she stood for a few moments looking at the shelves, then pulled a volume of poetry from the shelf and put it into her knapsack.

Mrs. Brandon had been gone a half hour and Julia started worrying that something had gone wrong, when at last she heard the sound of a coach and horses approaching. From the window she saw a four-wheeled coach pulled by two silvery-white horses driven by a coachman coming round the bend. The coach stopped in front of the house. Mrs. Brandon sat inside, looking as elegant as when her husband had been town mayor. The upper part of the coach was painted a shiny satiny black, the lower part was pea-green. The wheels were made of polished wood. The coachman wore blue and white livery. Yes, she and her mother would easily pass as gentry.

Relieved, Julia shouted goodbye to her father but

she didn't want to slow down long enough to run back and give him a hug, so she grabbed the bag she had packed and rushed out the door. Mrs. Brandon stepped down from the carriage and went to lock the front door. At last, Julia and her mother were seated in the coach facing each other. Julia sat in the seat riding backward. The seat facing backwards always made her mother feel a little uneasy, but Julia didn't mind it. Instead of seeing where they were going, she could see where they had been.

The coachman flicked the reins, and the harness bells jingled. The coach started moving, the horse hooves clipping on the road.

It was a perfect morning. The air was still and calm, the clouds high and white and fluffy with no sign of rain in any direction. Soon Julia became accustomed to the jostling of the carriage. The seats were cushioned, but not deeply enough to protect them from feeling each bump in the road. It had been so long since she'd ridden in a coach, she'd entirely forgotten to bring extra cushions.

"You know," said Julia. "I was thinking about what happened, and I am so sorry for my stubbornness and pride. I should have gone to London in search of a husband, as you wanted me to."

"You may have been right to refuse, Julia. I shouldn't have asked you to live a lie. But who can think straight when everything goes wrong all at once?"

"But look what I'm doing now, sneaking from Guildford Manor in the dead of night with gold which doesn't belong to me." She shuddered, thinking of it. "You called me selfish, and you were right."

"There is nothing selfish in what you are doing now," said Mrs. Brandon. "You have a great deal of courage, Julia. Let's just hope this turns out well."

"I never feel courageous." It was true, she didn't. Sitting in Lord Guildford's parlor the night before, for example, she'd been terrified–of accidentally saying something wrong, of him overpowering her, which he could easily do.

"You have a strong sense of decorum," said Mrs. Brandon, "and high ideals. Following your ideals gives you courage."

Julia looked out the window. She wondered if by now, perhaps, Lord Guildford noticed his gold was missing. She looked at the morning sky and supposed it was still too early. He used that parlor later in the afternoon and evenings. Now the family would be just gathering for breakfast. When he did discover the gold missing, he would probably call Mr. Ames and ask the house to be searched. She wondered how long Blanche and Cecilia would be able to hide her absence. Would Lord Guildford be deeply furious to find out she had been deceiving him when she'd promised to go riding with him and tell him all her secrets on Tuesday? It was difficult to imagine Lord Guildford angry. He always seemed so sunny and radiant. *He lives too much in the moment,* Cecilia had said. *Sometimes he doesn't like to look too deeply into matters or think too precisely about what he is doing or how people around him are really feeling.* This, of course, explained his treatment of Cecilia and his attitude toward Cecilia's tears. He probably just figured if he waited long enough, she'd snap out of it and be fine.

She hadn't told her parents the entire story, of course. She'd left out the parts about her and Lord Guildford.

Julia and Mrs. Brandon said little to each other as the coach bounced along over the road, which had become more heavily gutted now that they were on the larger highway. Because it was summer, the roads were passable. An occasional muddy ditch or bog was all that slowed the traffic. Julia was surprised by how many travelers there were. Many were on horseback, riding leisurely. Most travelers went by foot. There were a few beggars, mostly elderly people wandering from place to place, asking for alms. Occasionally they saw another coach coming the other way down the road. Also, on occasion, coaches going their direction passed them at higher speeds, usually larger, finer coaches pulled by four, or even six horses.

Generally the foot travelers scrambled out of the road when the coach approached, but three lads of about sixteen, who looked as if they were cottagers from a village like Burgess Hill, stayed on the road, causing the coachman to swerve dangerously to keep from hitting them. Both Julia and her mother looked back at the lads as they passed. "Foolish boys," Mrs. Brandon said.

For a while, Julia watched the passing countryside, the emerald green of the hills and the scattering of thatched cottages. Already the countryside was busy: the hay harvest had begun, with men gathering the hay into piles and women coming behind with hemp ropes to tie it into bundles. The donkey carts followed behind them, with other men loading the hay onto the cart.

Farmers leading their teams of oxen to the field were on the road. There were two milkmaids leading a cow by a rope. Another girl carried a basket of eggs on her arm.

Then she opened her knapsack and took out her book. She opened the book and flipped past Sir Philip Sidney's sonnets, past the lyrics of John Donne and Ben Johnson, past the passages from Richard Crawhaw and excerpts from Spencer's Fairy Queen. She checked the index and saw that the volume contained a few of Robert Herrick's poems. Finding the pages with Herrick's poetry, she read:

A sweet disorder in the dress
Kindles in clothes a wantonness:
A lawn about the shoulders thrown
Into a fine distraction–
An erring lace, which here and there
Enthralls the crimson stomacher–
A cuff neglectful, and thereby
Ribbands to flow confusedly–
A winning wave, deserving note,
In the tempestuous petticoat–
A careless shoe-string, in whose tie
I see a wild civility–
Do more bewitch me than when art
Is too precise in every part.

A poem extolling the virtues of imperfection? Once, she wouldn't have taken such a thing seriously. She would have said, better to repair the erring lace, bring the ribbands into order, tie the loose shoe-string. Now she read the poem again, trying not to immediately dismiss the notion as absurd. How well the poem conveyed the wild exhilarating freedom in letting go of perfection.

She closed the book on her lap, her finger holding the place, and looked out the window. She knew there were those who did not strive for perfection–her brother, Geoffrey, for one, was too governed by his passions. But to find charm in the imperfection itself. What an idea. She imagined Geoffrey would like the poem. She knew Lord Guildford would.

She opened the book again and read the next poem:

Have ye beheld (with much delight)
A red rose peeping through a white?
Or else a cherry (double graced)
Within a lily? Centre placed?
Or ever marked the pretty beam
A strawberry shows half drowned in cream?
Or seen rich rubies blushing through
A pure smooth pearl, and orient too?
So like to this, nay all the rest,
Is each neat niplet of Julia's breast.

She felt so embarrassed over this one, she had to close the book and turn her face away so her mother wouldn't see. She pressed her cheek to the glass, pretending to look outside.

Why would you send me one of Herrick's verses, she had asked Lord Guildford.

Because they are beautiful and because he writes about a lovely girl named Julia, he had said.

The memory returned to her of how Guildford

106

had touched her and kissed her that morning they'd gone riding. She felt trembly all over, and mistook the suddenly weak sensation in her limbs for fright.

Well, she certainly had good reason to be frightened, but what good would it do now, to worry? She was on her way to London with money stolen from Lord Guildford. For all she knew, this caper would land her in prison and this ride through the countryside would be her last taste of freedom for a long, long time. Worrying would do nothing but make her sick.

Once they reached Cranston, the road merged with the larger road to London. As they drew closer to the city, the villages were set more closely together, and the roads were more crowded.

As they neared London, her spirits rose. With great effort, she set aside her misgivings and apprehensions. There was nothing she could do now to alter the course on which she had set herself. Perhaps there was never much we could do to alter our courses. So what was there to do but admire the goldcup flowers which lay so thick and lush in the passing lanes, and the hillsides sparkling emerald in the sunlight?

When she let herself feel the beauty of the moment, when she accepted that she had no idea what was around the bend and she would never know until she rounded the bend, she felt, for just a moment, that Lord Guildford was right about one thing. All that was beautiful was only ours to borrow.

The sign announcing the Bell and Dragon was set atop a brick structure in the shape of an archway through which the coach entered the inn courtyard. There in the courtyard was a row of fine carriages and coaches, and a stable large enough for a few dozen horses.

The coachman pulled to a stop, and opened the door for Mrs. Brandon and Julia. "Yes," said Mrs. Brandon, looking up at the shuttered windows, "this inn will do nicely."

They alighted from the carriage. After so many hours being jostled and bounced along the road, Julia felt unsteady on her feet, the way a sailor must feel stepping on shore after a long time at sea.

Through a wrought-iron gate, they entered a smaller walled courtyard set with small smooth paving stones. At the center of the courtyard was a fountain surrounded by benches.

The landlord, who most have been alerted that a coach was approaching, came into the courtyard to greet them.

"I have a large room with a private sitting room," he said. "Perfect for two ladies traveling alone. The cost is three pounds for the night. The price includes a midday meal and light supper."

This was a great deal of money for a single night and a few meals–six weeks wages as a lady's maid at Guildford Manor.

"Perfect," said Mrs. Brandon. "We will take it. Thank you."

"This way, please," he said.

The main doors were large with pointed arches in the Gothic style, the door handles made of wrought iron. Just inside was a waiting area with chairs, a game table, and a fireplace. The interior smelled of rose petals and herbs and beeswax. The innkeeper led them up a staircase. The stairs and landing were carpeted. The inn was certainly luxurious.

At the top of the stairs was a door. The innkeeper took a skeleton key from his pocket, opened the door, and handed the key to Mrs. Brandon. He stood aside while Julia and Mrs. Brandon entered.

The room itself was spacious, with mahogany furniture and a large four-poster bed. The gleam of furniture and faint smell of lemons told Julia the room had been recently cleaned. The feather pillows on the bed were piled as high as Lady Cecilia's bed. The bed and windows were curtained. Beeswax candles so fragrant their scent filled the room, were set in pewter holders.

"We have a fine rose garden in the back," the inn keeper said, "and an orchard."

"Lovely," said Mrs. Brandon.

"I will send your midday meal up to your room," he said, "unless you ladies prefer to eat in the tavern."

"We prefer to eat here, thank you," said Mrs. Brandon.

The innkeeper bowed and left, promising to send a tray up to them right away.

Julia went into the adjoining sitting room and sat in one of the chairs by the window. The shutters were open but the windows were so heavily leaded she could not see out. She suspected that if she could, she'd be able to see over the courtyard wall to the street. How good it felt to sit in a chair instead of bouncing over the open road or the cobblestones of the city. She closed her eyes, feeling the exhaustion of the night before.

Soon a servant knocked on the door with a tray of spiced cold meats and bread made with herbs. Julia and her mother ate in the sitting room. Mrs. Brandon ate quickly, eager to be on her way. When she finished, she stood up, and dabbed her mouth with her kerchief.

"I will send word back as soon as I have news. Meanwhile you had so little sleep last night, you might like a nap. There should be no reason at all for you to leave the inn. If the gardens in the back are walled, they should be safe, but please use good judgment. And do not go into the front courtyard."

"Yes, Mama."

Julia followed her mother to the door. When her mother was gone and the door closed behind her, Julia took the key from the table and locked the door. She felt safe–for the moment.

It was early afternoon and the day's work was done. Robert Guildford had met with the managers of the estates and his uncle's solicitor, he had approved the month's financial reports, and ordered the necessary repairs in the family's London townhouse.

He entered his private parlor. First thing he did upon entering was check the chairs to make sure nobody was in them. Never again would he blithely assume a room was empty simply because he didn't see anybody. The dish of chocolates and bottle of sauterne had been returned to the side table, and someone had washed the glasses and returned them to the cabinet. The straight-backed chairs, however, had been left where he had placed them, pulled away from the wall and grouped together around a curtained table.

He sat in the chair in which Julia had been sitting. It was then he noticed the empty dish on the larger table under the window–the Meissen porcelain dish which, the night before, had contained the gold coins his solicitor had placed there. Startled, he looked around to see if perhaps he'd confused the dishes, and the coins were elsewhere in the room.

He sat up straight, trying to think of who might have removed the coins without telling him. The fleeting thought came to him that the coins had been stolen, but he immediately rejected the possibility. Never, as far as he knew, had anything ever been stolen from his house.

A soft knock came at the door.

"Enter," he said.

The butler, Ames, entered. "My lord, I have come to acquaint you with an unusual occurrence."

Guildford waited. Ames said, "Julia Dale, Lady Cecilia's personal lady's maid, seems to have left the house. It appears she has left permanently."

Bells of alarm were ringing in his head. He remembered Julia had looked briefly at the coins in the dish. *When you learn my secret you will cast me from your house,* she had said.

Was Julia, the girl with the sweetest face he'd ever seen, a common thief?

"Where has she gone?"

"I have been unable to discover that. This

morning she did not come to breakfast. Cecilia and Blanche said she was ill, but after the mid-day meal, a chambermaid discovered it was not Julia in her bed but pillows under the covers intended to look like her. The chambermaid became frightened and told me."

"Where do you think she has gone?"

"I believe she has left carrying letters for Lady Cecilia. I believe this because she sent a letter to a certain John and Alice in Burgess Hill."

"Who are John and Alice in Burgess Hill?"

"It could be a coincidence of names, but I was recently informed that Geoffrey Brandon's parents are also named John and Alice."

"What did my sister say about Julia's disappearance?"

"She isn't saying much."

"I will go speak to her myself," he said.

He found Cecilia sitting at her dressing table. "Good day, Robert," she said calmly when he entered. Now he knew something was up involving her. His highly emotional sister was never calm. She watched him in the mirror.

"Where has Julia gone?"

"I do not know."

She was lying.

"Tell me the truth, Cecilia."

"Is that a command, my tyrannical brother?"

"Cecilia," he used his most authoritative tone, "you will tell me where Julia is, and what she is doing."

Now she lifted her chin and looked straight at him in the mirror. "I believe she has gone home for a short visit."

He didn't bother asking why, then, she and Blanche put pillows in her bed and tried to hide her departure. Instead he said, "You are lying to me Cecilia. Please tell me where she has gone."

"You will find out."

"When? On Tuesday, perhaps?"

A look of amusement crossed her face. So she knew about Julia's promise to meet him on Tuesday and tell all.

"There was a dish of gold coins in my parlor."

"Yes," she said evenly, "there was."

"They are not there any more. Where are they?"

From the way Cecilia hesitated, he knew she was trying to decide what to tell him. She said, "The truth is that I don't know where they are at this precise moment."

"Has Julia stolen gold from this house?"

"No, she has not. I took the gold and gave it to her."

"What I believe," said Guildford, watching her face, "is that Julia is smuggling a letter to your lover in his prison cell."

He knew from the way her eyes widened slightly that this was what was happening. He tried to imagine Julia leaving her position and going all the way to London, by herself with fifty pounds in gold for the purpose of delivering a love letter.

It just didn't make sense. There had to be something more.

To get Cecilia to talk, he said, "There is nothing I can do about our father's will."

"As if you'd let me marry who I wanted, even if it were up to you." There. Now some of the fire was back in her eyes. Ames' guess had been correct. Whatever was going on had something to do with Geoffrey Brandon.

He remembered the day he'd caught Cecilia with her lover. The image came back to him now, how they'd scrambled to cover themselves when he'd entered the room. He remembered the unwavering way Geoffrey Brandon had looked at him.

"He's fortune hunter, Cecilia."

"He is not."

"How do you know?"

"I know because he loves me."

Love? What he felt, hearing the passion in her voice, was scorn.

Seeing he wasn't going to get anything further from Cecilia, he turned on his heel and marched from the room. He found Sam Mason at the foot of the stairs. "Where is Blanche?"

"I believe she is in the garden, your lordship."

He strode down the marbled corridor to the wide doors leading to the gardens. He found Blanche on her knees clipping lavender and putting the sprigs into a basket. "Blanche," he said.

She must not have heard him approaching because she gave such a start she dropped her clippers.

She looked up at him, then sprang to her feet. "Your lordship!"

"Blanche, tell me. Do you know where Julia is?"

It did not take Blanche long to recover herself. "She is feeling ill, I believe."

Guildford shook his head in disgust. Now wouldn't you think Blanche and Cecilia could at least be organized enough to get their stories straight?

"Ill?" he said. "Is it serious?"

She crinkled her nose mischievously and smiled at him. "Nothing serious, my lord. I believe she has a feminine ailment. She will be fine in a few days." There was a twinkle in her eye.

"Feminine ailment indeed. She has stolen from the house, and has taken with her a considerable amount of gold."

"Well, then," said Blanche, not at all surprised. "My lord," she put her hands together and held them to her breast. "In Julia's unfortunate absence, if you need someone to go riding with you on Tuesday, I'd be happy to join you. Or we can go now, should that please you better. You may find me more accommodating than the icy Julia."

She was teasing him. She was actually teasing him. A maid in his own house dared look him in the eye and tell a bald faced lie, then tease him.

He turned and without another word, walked away.

Sam Mason was waiting for him just inside. "My lord, did Blanche tell you where Julia has gone?"

"She did not. They are in confederacy, all three of them. Perhaps you should go out and talk to her. Maybe she will tell you what she would not tell me. I can assure you, Sam, if you are able to learn what is going on, I shall reward you richly."

Mostly Guildford felt off balance. He'd been so sure of himself, feeling like the spider who had the fly trapped safely in his web. He knew she'd been up to something, but it had never occurred to him that she might steal away from the house, taking his gold with her.

115

He went to his office and rang for the butler. When Ames entered, Guildford gave orders. "I will need ten of the best horses saddled and ready to go, and nine horsemen, all good strong riders."

"Yes, your lordship."

"Tell the riders to prepare for a few nights away. If you have any messages for me in the next few days, you can send them to me at the London townhouse. I will send word back if my whereabouts change. See to it now. I will meet the riders at the stables shortly."

Just then, a knock came at the door. It was Harry, the master of his horses.

"Yes, Harry?"

"A horse is missing, your lordship, a gray mare belonging to Lady Cecilia."

So Julia had gone by horseback. That meant by now, she could be in London, and already accomplished whatever she'd set out to do, which would explain why Cecilia and Blanche were so pert with him.

Mr. Ames said, "Your lordship, shall I call the authorities and have her tracked down? If she has taken a horse–?"

"There is no need to involve the authorities," said Guildford.

"What then, my lord, do you plan to do?" asked Ames.

"I will search for her myself. I will begin in Burgess Hill, with John and Alice."

There was something Guildford needed to do before he could leave. He found his great-uncle, the earl, in his private library, sitting in a chair near a window with his feet on a stool. The earl was looking out the window, his face utterly calm. Ever since he'd abdicated the responsibilities of ruling the estates, his face seemed almost angelically calm. From the chair in which he sat, he could see over the back gardens, all the way to the orchards.

"Uncle," Guildford said, entering the room. The earl looked at him, but said nothing. It was often hard to read anything in the old man's face.

"Julia Dale, the maid you met yesterday evening in my parlor, has left the house."

The earl nodded his head, as if he already knew. He pointed out the window, toward the orchard. Guildford waited to see if he was going to say more. At last, he pointed and said, "Just after midnight, she went there."

Just after midnight? She'd left the house within hours of leaving his parlor?

"Why didn't you tell anyone?"

He waited, but the earl said nothing.

"The butler, Ames, believes she is carrying smuggled letters to Cecilia's lover in Newcastle."

Again, the earl didn't speak, so Guildford said, "It is not my choice, of course. My father's will and the disposition of Cecilia's dowry is beyond my control. If it were up to me, I would not be opposed to Cecilia choosing her own husband. But I do not approve of that one."

The earl studied him carefully for several minutes. Guildford waited. At last, the earl said, "Why?"

"I don't believe he loves her. And I don't like him." But then he remembered the way Geoffrey had looked at him at the start of their duel, when Geoffrey must have known, from the expert way

Guildford handled a sword, that he was going to lose. When Guildford knocked his sword from his hand, deeply slashing his arm in the process, he still showed no fear, even though Guildford could easily have killed him. Now Guildford wondered what sort of man faces what might be his last few moments of life without fear.

Robert Guildford and his ten horsemen assembled near the stables. "All right," he said, "listen to instructions. You three–" he pointed, "go to London and check to see if Geoffrey Brandon is in his cell at Newcastle. After you have learned what the situation is there, return to the London Townhouse and wait for further instructions. The others, we are riding to Burgess Hill."

He checked his pocket watch, then he and his troop of riders set off, galloping down the hill from Guildford Manor. As he rode, he imagined Julia traveling this same way, on Cecilia's mare. He could not fathom why she would risk everything, including her position, to deliver a letter.

They galloped the entire seven miles to Burgess Hill, arriving less than twenty minutes later. Guildford, who rode in the lead, slowed as they approached the village. He stopped to greet the first man he saw, a red-haired man guiding a vegetable cart pulled by a donkey.

"Excuse me, my good man," Guildford said, touching the brim of his hat. "Can you tell me where I might find two people by the name of John and

Alice?"

"Yes, sir. That would be John and Alice Brandon. They live in the gray stone cottage at the end of this street," he said, pointing.

John and Alice Brandon. So it was not a coincidence of names.

"Can you also tell me if a girl named Julia Dale lives in this village?"

"There's nobody by the name of Dale in this village. There's Julia Brandon, John and Alice's daughter."

So great was Guildford's shock, he felt something like a rush of dizziness.

"She's gone, though," said the man, "to serve as a maid in the–" he stopped and gave Lord Guildford a closer look. "Well, by gosh, aren't you Lord Guildford?"

The man was waiting for a response, so Guildford drew in his breath to steady himself and said, "Yes, I am Robert Guildford."

"Then you must know Julia Brandon! A very pretty girl."

"Blue eyes, and brown hair?" Guildford asked, still hoping there was some mistake of identity."

"Yes, my lord. That would be her."

"Thank you for the information." Guildford tipped his hat and turned his horse away. So she was Julia Brandon. Now he knew something more was going on than the delivery of a love letter. Had she entered his household as a spy? Had she taken him for a fool from the moment she'd entered his house? For the first time, he felt his anger rising.

He rode in the direction of the gray stone cottage at the end of the street. There, in the stable of the neighboring house, was Cecilia's gray mare. A young girl sat on the neighbor's front stoop, playing with a fox-eared puppy. In the yard a boy of about ten was scattering seeds for the hens.

Guildford walked up the path to the gray stone cottage, aware that the girl on the neighboring stoop was watching him. He knocked at the Brandon's door. There was no answer. He knocked again harder. From inside came the barking of a dog, but there was still no answer. The shutters were closed and the house appeared dark.

He crossed the lawn to the neighbor's door. "Is your mother or father here?" he asked the girl.

The girl leapt up and opened the door and called inside, "Mama! A gentleman is here. I think he's looking for Mr. Brandon!"

"Coming," came a woman's shout from within the house. Then a woman of about thirty, her head wrapped in a cloth, came onto the porch.

"My lord," she said, evidently surprised by the sight of him. He wondered if she knew who he was.

"Greetings," he said, "I'd like to ask you a few questions." She waited, so he said, "That gray mare in your stables. Whose horse is that?"

"That horse belongs to the Guildfords. We're taking care of it for now until it can be returned."

"I see," he said. "Your neighbors, John and Alice Brandon–" he gestured toward the gray stone cottage. "I knocked, but there was no answer."

"You'll never get an answer, sir. Mr. Brandon was thrown from a horse and hasn't recovered. He's confined to a chair."

"Where is his wife? And his daughter, Julia?"

"His wife and daughter set out in a fine carriage

bound for London this morning. Naturally, John couldn't go because of his back."

"When did they leave?"

"Just after daybreak."

"I see. Can you describe the carriage?"

The woman thought for a minute. "It was black, yes. The top half was black, the bottom half green."

"Very good. I would like to speak to Mr. Brandon. Someone must be able to get into the house, if he's bound in a chair."

"Yes, sir. I have a key to the back door. I check in on him, and with his wife gone, I'll be bringing his meals."

"I have not properly introduced myself," said Guildford. "My name is Robert Guildford, I am–"

"Lord Guildford!" she bobbed a quick curtsy. "Then the horse belongs to you! I will get the key and take you to the Brandon's home. You may certainly come in and wait, if you like."

"I will wait out here, thank you."

He waited on the front porch while she went into the house. She came back a few minutes later carrying a skeleton key. He followed her across her front yard. A white picket fence separating her yard from the Brandon's yard was low enough for her to pick up her skirts and step over.

He called to his riders, "Three of you," he pointed, "you, you, and you. Come with me."

The three riders dismounted and joined him as he followed the woman to the back of the Brandon's house. The woman walked around to the back door, and rapped loudly. "John!" she shouted. "I'm coming in, and bringing a visitor!"

She unlocked the door, and stepped inside.

Guildford followed, ducking his head so he wouldn't hit his forehead against the low door frame. Inside, he found himself in a small kitchen dominated by a large hooded fireplace surrounded by pegs on which hung pots, pans, and utensils. A chimney shelf was lined with jugs and jars. One door led to a large pantry. The woman opened another door leading to a front common room containing a small dining area with a trestle table and two benches.

Guildford followed her. His three men followed him.

"John!" the woman called. "Are you awake?"

"Over here," he said, "in the bedroom."

The woman turned to Guildford and gestured toward a door.

"Thank you," he said. "I can find my way from here."

The doorframe to the bedroom, also, was so low Guildford had to stoop to enter. His men waited just outside while he went in. The room was narrow, no more than ten paces across, the walls in need of paint. The floors were wood, but scuffed and scratched.

In a chair with his foot on a stool sat a man of about sixty years. His hair was a soft misty gray with a dignified streak of black at his temples. His face was lined, his expression gentle. His eyes were a deep sapphire blue.

"Welcome to my home, my lord," Mr. Brandon said. "Forgive me for being unable to rise."

John Brandon, who spoke like a well-bred and well-educated gentleman, had evidently seen better days. He had the sort of eyes that crinkled kindly when he talked. If this was Julia's father, it was no wonder her manners were so dignified. Guildford was aware of the water stains on the walls and ceilings. This man did not belong in this house.

"Please, don't even think of rising," Guildford said. "I quite understand."

"There is a chair, over there," Mr. Brandon said, pointing. "Please make yourself comfortable."

Guildford pulled the chair from the wall and placed it not far from Mr. Brandon and sat down. "I am Robert Guildford," he said.

"Yes," said Mr. Brandon. "I guessed as much."

Guildford wondered how much Mr. Brandon knew. "If you know who I am, you probably know why I have come."

"Whatever your reason for honoring me with a visit, I would like to take the opportunity to apologize for the behavior of my headstrong and rash son."

For the moment, Guildford thought it best to delicately change the subject. Given Mr. Brandon's poise, Guildford didn't believe for a moment he would willingly tell him where his wife and daughter and gone or what they were up to. The best strategy, he felt, was to circle around the subject.

"Have you lived long in this cottage?"

"No, my lord. Until a few months ago, I was mayor of Worthing. Then came the scandals. Trying to save my son from prison cost much money. I lost my post because of the whispers of theft, and worse."

"I see." Then Guildford asked what he most wanted to know: "When your daughter Julia entered service in my house," he spoke slowly and deliberately, "did she know that my sister, Lady Cecilia, was the lady Geoffrey-" He stopped. He couldn't bring himself to say the word 'loved,' not here, in this room, with the man who was father to both Geoffrey Brandon and Julia.

"I am quite sure she did not know."

"How are you so sure?"

"Because none of us knew a lady had been involved at all. Geoffrey did not tell me the details, and I assumed it was a gambling quarrel, or some other sort of tavern brawl. I knew a certain Lord Howard challenged Geoffrey to a duel, and that Geoffrey was injured. I knew there had been a quarrel of some kind, but I never inquired into the particulars of the quarrel. My son was fortunate not to have been killed. Challenging noblemen to duels! Of all the foolish things to do."

Guildford sensed the man was telling the truth. "Your son fought bravely," Guildford said. He didn't mention that he'd been the one to fight him.

Mr. Brandon smiled, but it was a sad, wry smile. "Sometimes there is a fine line between bravery and stupidity."

Guildford sat back in his chair. This conversation was not going at all as he expected. This man, father to both Julia and Geoffrey Brandon, was the picture of calm gentility. Then it occurred to him that Mr. Brandon could also be a smooth liar. He had good reason, after all, in this particular moment, not to be truthful.

"Why did your daughter enter service at Guildford House?" he asked.

"Because yours is the grandest household in the vicinity which would provide the best opportunities for service. And because, in her quiet way, she is as stubborn as her brother."

"I don't understand."

Mr. Brandon looked Guildford directly in the eye and said, "To tell you truly, her mother had a different plan for her, a plan which Julia rejected."

"What plan was that?"

"We were still in our house in Worthing. Her mother wanted to send Julia to London to stay with acquaintances for the season, dressed in borrowed clothing and jewels, hoping to find a gentleman who could marry her and offer a better lifestyle than appeared to be in our future."

He imagined Julia dressed in fine clothing and jewels, appearing at London social events. "I am sure she would have had suitors, and probably marriage offers as well. Why did Julia reject this plan?"

"The plan required hiding the, er, reduced circumstances of our family. Julia insisted she could not deceive or trap a future husband. Like her brother, she believes marriage should be based in love."

"I see."

"Your horse is in the neighbor's stable," said Mr. Brandon, "and your gold will be returned to you. I consider the debt to be my son's. If he is unable to return it, I will find a way to give it back."

"Mr. Brandon, I will forgive the debt, but I would like for you to tell me where in London your wife and daughter have gone."

Mr. Brandon sat back, considering this. "I thought my son Geoffrey a rash and impulsive fool when I learned that he'd dueled with a man of rank and angered a family of wealth and power. I understand the grave risk I am taking now in not answering your question, but I really cannot tell you. Please understand I have my wife and daughter's safety to consider."

Guildford expected such an answer. He considered offering a bargain of some sort, but Mr. Brandon would have no reason to trust him. His uncles would resort to threats, but Guildford didn't have the heart just then for threats.

So he said, "I do know they have gone to London. I have sent two of my men to Newcastle Prison, because I assume that is where they can be intercepted."

"It doesn't matter, then, what I say or do not say."

For several long seconds, they watched each other's eyes. Then Guildford said, "I'd best be going then."

He stood up and turned to go. Mr. Brandon stopped him by quietly saying, "My lord?"

Guildford turned back.

"My daughter was in your house, so you may already know this. She is a an extraordinary person. She has great strength of character. However, she is a defenseless young woman who may now be separated from her mother. May I ask you, as a man of honor, if you find her to see that she is protected."

Guildford nodded his head. "Yes, I will see that she is protected."

His men were waiting just outside the door. He walked past them, and, in a few long strides, crossed the common room. He opened the front door, and exited. His men followed.

Once they reached the road, one of his men laughed quietly. "You will see that she is protected, my lord? The way a cat will protect a mouse?"

At the pace they were galloping, Guildford supposed he and his riding party would be in London within two hours, but Julia and her mother had almost a full day's head start. Most likely, he was too late to stop whatever they were planning.

Guildford was a strong rider. A two hour gallop was nothing to him. They paused only to refresh the horses. It was late afternoon when they arrived at the Guildford Townhouse in London. The two men he'd sent ahead to the prison were there, waiting for them.

"What have you learned?" Guildford asked them.

"Geoffrey Brandon was not in his cell," one of them said. "He'd requested a special hearing with the magistrate. He claimed to have letters proving his innocence."

"Letters? What sort of letters?"

"Letters from Lady Cecilia swearing Geoffrey had never abducted her, that she'd gone with him willingly."

Guildford sank into a chair. "She put this in a letter which she is willing to make public?"

Nobody answered. Of course his sister Cecilia was fully capable of such a thing. His first thought was this would make it impossible to arrange a decent marriage for her. His second thought was that this may have been her design. At least he knew now what this caper was all about.

"Where is everyone now?"

"We believe Geoffrey is still in the office of the magistrate. The magistrate examined the letters he presented, and has ordered Lady Cecilia to London so he can determine whether the letters are genuine. The magistrate said Geoffrey will not be returned to his cell until the matter can be resolved."

"My sister is on her way to London?"

"She has been summoned. Whether she is on her way, I do not know."

"Was Julia at this special hearing?"

"No, my lord. Her mother was there, but Julia was not."

"Where is she?"

"Nobody knows. Well, I'm sure her mother knows, but I rather doubt she'll tell us."

"They came in a coach," Guildford said, "a black and green coach. Did you see it?"

"Yes, my lord. I saw a coach matching that description in front of the magistrate's court room."

Guildford wanted to find Julia, desperately. His reason now was different from the reason he'd had when he'd started out. *You know how to play,* his sister Cecilia had flung at him not long after their uncles had Geoffrey imprisoned, *you know how to dance and make sport, but you don't like to think.* At the time, he'd dismissed her accusation as nonsense. As it happened, he'd been one of the finest scholars in his university class. Of course he liked to think.

But be could plainly see he hadn't done enough thinking.

That girl, his great-uncle the earl had said, *has a rare spirit.*

"All right," Guildford said. "What we will do now is find Julia. We will split up." He rang for the townhouse butler, and asked for a map of London. When the map was brought, he assigned each of his men a different region.

"She may be hidden with relatives, but on such notice and under such circumstances she's most likely at an inn. Inquire at every inn. They took a great deal of gold with them, so she is probably at a fine inn. It is unlikely they have given their real names, so ask discretely whether two women, one older and one younger, are there. Watch for her on the street, as well, but I doubt she'll be out on the street. We will meet back here in one hour."

Julia awakened from her nap with a jolt and sat up. Instantly she remembered where she was, but she had no idea how long she had been sleeping. She rose from the bed, washed in the basin, put on her dress. The lace was badly in need of pressing and the ribbon which tied the bodice so crumpled nothing but an iron would smooth it out. Her braids had fallen loose. Instead of rebraiding her hair, she tied her hair loosely with a ribbon and let it fall down her back. She looked in the mirror, and saw, in Herrick's words, a sweet disorder.

She suspected from how close and warm the air felt that it was late afternoon. She considered trying to open a window for fresh air, but thought instead she would go downstairs and walk in the garden.

That was when she saw that a sealed note had been slipped under her door. She opened it and read:

Dearest Julia,
I am sending a few lines back to you with the

coachman, who will deliver this letter and return to me.

Geoffrey sends his most heartfelt thanks. By early afternoon, we were able to get a hearing with the magistrate, who read Lady Cecilia's letter and agreed that if it is genuine and not a forgery, there would be no grounds for a charge of abduction against Geoffrey. The magistrate said the charge of abduction was serious indeed, and in fact, was a hanging crime. So he gave the order for Lady Cecilia to be summoned immediately from Guildford House so he could determine whether in fact she wrote the letter. I believe if the Guildford family does not bring her, the magistrate will find the charges against Geoffrey unfounded and release him immediately.

I shall stay here with Geoffrey until she arrives, which I assume will be before nightfall.

I instructed the coachman to slide this note under the door if you do not answer to a soft knock because I know you may be napping.

Written at about two o'clock.

Julia felt exhilarated. For the first time since leaving Guildford Manor, she believed the plan might really work.

She left the room, locked her door behind her, and put the key into her waistband. The corridor and staircase was deserted. Once downstairs, she heard voices and quiet laughter coming from the tavern, which was separated from the main part of the inn by a door set with windows. Across the waiting area was a heavy gothic-style door. She pushed it open and found herself on a back patio. It was later than she'd supposed. The sun had already dipped below the horizon.

Beyond the patio were the rose gardens consisting of beds of roses, fruit trees, and tall hedges in need of trimming. The gardens were not symmetrical and regular like the well-manicured gardens at Guildford Manor. The crocuses and lilies and marigolds were planted together in a jumble. The path meandered through the rose beds. Here and there were benches and fountains. Flowering vines grew wild on the garden walls. She could hear, from beyond the walls, the sounds from the streets–shouts, cartwheels, the braying of donkeys. The sound of horses and donkeys and creaking cartwheels added to the sense of restlessness in this garden. She thought that here, too, to harrow another of Herrick's phrases, was a wild civility.

At the far end of the gardens, just before the start of the orchards, was a bench hidden from view of the inn by an ivy-covered wall. The bench was pushed up against the wall so Julia could sit and lean back. How strange it felt to sit in a garden in the midst of the city, close enough to hear the sounds, separated by high walls. It seemed right that the garden was a disorganized jumble.

She sat with her head tipped back and her eyes closed. She could smell the water in the fountains, and the scent of cut grass.

What would happen next, she had no idea. She supposed, but did not know for sure, that Geoffrey would be freed from prison. She hoped, but dared not feel too certain, that her father be restored to his former position, and would not have to live his last years in a broken down cottage on the edge of Burgess Hill.

On the other hand, it was entirely possible that the plan could still go dreadfully wrong. Cecilia's uncles would not like being bested, and might cause more mischief. Better to keep her expectations in check.

She must have sat back with her eyes closed for a very long time because when she opened her eyes, dusk had further darkened the sky, creating deep shadows in the orchard.

Startled, she saw a man standing not far away. He wore a powdered wig and white silken shirt with lace on the cuffs and collar. She sat up straight, her heart suddenly pounding. She'd never seen this man before in her life, but he was smiling at her familiarly, as if he knew who she was.

"Sir!" she said, thoroughly alarmed.

"I am sorry to frighten you, my dear," he said. "My name is Mr. Moncrief."

Her mind was racing, but she could not recall ever having heard that name before.

"And what is your name?" he asked politely.

"I am–" she looked helplessly toward the inn. Then, fighting to compose herself, she said, "I know nobody by the name of Moncrief."

"We have never met before," he said. "Much the pity. You are, without a doubt, the most beautiful girl I have ever seen."

It occurred to her that he thought she was a prostitute. After all, she was alone at an inn. She flushed with embarrassment.

She stood up. "I must be getting back inside, sir."

"Wait!" he said, and moved to block her so she could not leave. He then softened his command by saying, "Please. I don't know who you are, or why you are here, but I am willing to offer you three hundred pounds if you will stay with me tonight."

She was so astonished it was a moment before she could take in his meaning.

"No, indeed! You very much mistake me. Please let me pass."

"Perhaps you do not understand how much money I am offering you."

"I do. I understand. Three hundred pounds is a fortune. But my answer is no. Please let me pass."

"I really cannot let you go. Perhaps if I raise the offer–"

"No, sir!" Her alarm was deepening. "Please let me go–"

This stranger, this Mr. Moncrief, reached out and grasped her arm, not tightly enough to hurt her, but tightly enough so that she could not pull away.

Her heart was racing and she was so frightened she felt dizzy. She drew in her breath to scream when a voice from near the hedge said, "The lady said no, and I believe she means no."

Mr. Moncrief still held her arm, but she could twist herself far enough to see that the speaker was Lord Guildford.

"Lord Guildford!" she cried.

Guildford looked calmly at the man and said, "Let go of the lady's arm."

It was the same tone he had used the morning on the road, when she was on her way to take up her post as lady's maid at Guildford Manor, when his friends had made sport with her.

"I said let go of the lady's arm," Guildford said. "Now."

Through her shock, Julia was aware that Guildford referred to her as a lady. She felt weak with gratitude.

Mr. Moncrief let go of her arm.

"Are you all right, Julia?" Guildford asked her.

"Yes," she said, rubbing her arm where Mr. Moncrief had gripped her. Her heart was still pounding wildly and she was afraid she might lose her balance.

To Mr. Moncrief, Guildford said, "Please leave us."

"Certainly, my lord. Accept my humble apologies. I meant no harm." He bowed with an exaggerated flourish of his wrist, and turned and walked briskly around the corner and disappeared from view. Julia was not surprised at the man's reaction: Lord Guildford, as always, presented a splendid and impressive figure.

She turned to face him, drawing herself up to her full height, startled by his somber expression. There was such a heaviness, almost a stricken melancholy about him, she actually felt alarmed. She'd never seen him without a twinkle in his eye and hint of laughter in his face.

She could think of only one explanation for his melancholy. "Have you come to arrest me for theft, my lord?"

"No, Julia," he said quietly. He said nothing more. There was a question, and a sense of helplessness in his eyes, as if he were at a loss for words. This, too, was something new. She would never have imagined the great Lord Guildford at a loss for words.

She remembered how his family had exaggerated the charges against Geoffrey. She should have felt frightened now, but she felt no fear at all, even though they were alone in a garden growing dark near an orchard growing darker. In fact, she felt entirely equal to him.

"You have come to arrest me for something worse, then?" She heard the playful note in her own voice. She knew from his manner that, indeed, he had not come to accuse her of any crime.

"I have not come to arrest you at all. I have come to apologize."

"Apologize?" Nothing could have surprised her more.

"I did not set out to apologize this afternoon when I left Guildford Manor, but by mid-journey, my purpose changed. I am here to ask you to forgive me."

She shouldn't believe him. She should suspect him of lying or laying some snare for her, but in his voice was a humble ring of truth. He was genuinely sorry. Then she wondered if his change of attitude was, perhaps, because Cecilia had triumphed and Geoffrey had been set free. "Has Cecilia arrived yet in London?" she asked.

"I have no idea. I did not wait to find out. I have been too busy searching for you."

He stood back, at least five or six paces away. He did not step toward her, as she would have expected. Perhaps it was the physical distance between them which gave her more courage. Whatever the reason, she looked directly into his face with a boldness she would not have dared while in his house.

"Thank you for making that man leave," she said. "You protected me once before, on the road, when I was walking to Guildford Manor."

"I thought you were the most beautiful creature I'd ever seen."

A warm, delicious feeling came over her, leaving her feeling weak and breathless. *I must warn you about my brother,* Lady Cecilia had said. But now, for once, Julia had no desire to listen to words of caution.

Softly she said, "And I thought you were magnificent. So chivalrous, so–" she stopped, amazed by her own boldness. She had been about to say, *so handsome.*

She looked at his shoulders and remembered how it had felt to have his arms around her. Her heart was beating quickly, but she still felt no fear. She looked at his hands and remembered the way he had touched her the morning they'd gone riding, and her heart pounded even more wildly. *Is this not love?* She wanted to tell him she had an answer now to his question, a different answer than she had before, but instead of speaking, she smiled at him. He seemed startled by her smile.

"What are you thinking, Julia?" he asked, his voice not much more than a whisper.

"I'm thinking, what's to come is still unsure."

They both stood still. The next line of the poem hung in the air, unspoken.

In delay there lies no plenty.

In that moment, standing in this garden, looking into his face, at his somber expression devoid of his usual laughter and mirth, she didn't care what was to come. She cared only how she felt right now, in this moment. For all she knew, she would never again in her life feel the exquisiteness of what she was now feeling, a sensation which quickened her pulse and brought something like laughter rising in her chest.

She took a step forward, toward him. Then another.

Later, Guildford wasn't sure how it happened. He certainly had not come with the intention of taking her into his arms. But here she was, in his arms, the length of her body pressing against him. How thrilling, after desiring her for so long, to hold her close and breathe in her musky scent.

His lips were on hers, and her mouth was opened to him. His hands moved as if of their own will, circling her back, then her buttocks. She was all softness and curves and sweetness. He wanted her so badly all he felt was the ache of wanting her.

He felt her body ripple with laughter.

"Tell me," he whispered.

"I understand it now," she whispered back. "Why a girl would risk everything for a moment of love."

She pressed against him again. He held her tightly, rubbing her back and shoulders, urging the gown to fall lower, exposing more of her flesh. He lowered his head, kissing first her neck, then, tipping her back in his arms, her breasts. He ran his hands over her waist, then to her thighs. They were in shadows, but someone could come. He scooped her up and carried her deeper into the shadows of the orchards so they were entirely hidden from the walkway. He stopped when he felt the soft and springy grass underfoot. First set her down, then he put his jacket on the grass. Gently laid her down on the jacket, all the while kissing her mouth.

A voice in his head told him to stop, that she deserved better than to be taken like this, in the orchard of a common inn. But she was touching his neck and back. Her touch stripped away whatever willpower he might have had.

Impatiently he unbuttoned his shirt, shocked and delighted to feel her hands on his bare chest. He pushed aside her chemise. He wanted to go slow, to savor each moment, but urgency overcame him. Her breathing quickened as he caressed her. His hand was now on her thigh, pushing aside the fabric of her skirt until he found her bare leg.

Then she went stiff in his arms. He stopped and waited.

She pressed her cheek against his chest and breathed deeply again, relaxing against him, her breath warm. She moved her hips slightly. The movement was maddening. He touched her leg again, reaching higher. In one quick motion, he tugged aside her pantalets. With his knees, he pushed her legs apart.

There were no thoughts in Julia's head at all. None. Even the little voice which so frequently admonished her to do what was right and chastised her when she was wrong was now silent. A feeling of trembling warmth rushed through her. She gave herself over entirely to the sensations in her body.

Then they were both startled by a loud clanging and what sounded like a coach approaching the inn.

Julia bolted to a sitting position. "Oh, dear lord! It could be my mother."

They were on their feet. He helped her brush bits of grass and twigs from her hair. Hurriedly they pulled their clothing into place. She retied the ribbon around her hair and checked to make sure the brooch was in place.

"You go," he said. "I'll stay back, and follow behind."

She picked up her skirts and hurried from the orchard to the garden path. She entered the back door of the inn and saw her mother upstairs on the landing, knocking on their door.

"Mama! I'm here! What happened? How is Geoffrey?"

"Oh, Julia!" her mother was flushed with happiness. Julia ran up the stairs, but stopped at the landing, afraid if she drew too near, her mother would somehow guess what she had been doing not long before.

"Tell me! Is he free?" Julia said.

Her mother walked down the stairs, toward her. "Geoffrey is at the Guildford Townhouse. You've been summoned as well." Then the worst happened. Mrs. Brandon looked closely at her and said, "Are you all right?"

"I'm fine, Mama. I just ran up the stairs! I'm out of breath! Why have I been summoned? By whom?"

"The earl himself has come to London. He wants to meet Geoffrey, and he has summoned you. I fear it could be a trick, but Geoffrey is there and seems unconcerned. I met Lady Cecilia as well. A lovely young lady."

"The earl? Here in London?"

"You know that family now better than any of us. Do you think this could be a trick, a snare of some sort? Why would the earl be calling you to his townhouse, particularly after the things that have happened."

"I have no idea. Who else is there? Have Cecilia's uncles come?"

"No, there are no uncles. There seem to be cousins and other family members, but other than the earl, nobody seemed to be taking charge, and nobody was making Geoffrey uncomfortable. Lady Cecilia brought a maid with her, and a few servants to attend her." Mrs. Brandon paused to bite her lower lip. "I don't think calling us to their townhouse can be a trick, with so many people there. What do you think?"

"If the earl is there, but the uncles are not, I don't believe there is any trick."

"I suppose not. Cecilia is freely telling people that she took the gold from Lord Guildford's parlor."

She knew without looking that Guildford was somewhere nearby, where he could hear. She did not turn around.

"Then we don't have to worry about being accused of theft," said Julia.

"No. Besides, the magistrate understands that the root of all this was the family's attempt to keep Cecilia from marrying beneath her. So, then, I guess we should go. The coach is waiting outside. When we are on our way, I will tell you everything."

Julia followed Mrs. Brandon down the stairs. She looked back toward the garden, but the door was closed and she didn't see Guildford anywhere. Her mother walked through the waiting area, and out the front door. Julia followed. She looked back just before exiting the inn, but still didn't see him.

For just a moment she had the strangest sensation that she had imagined everything–Guildford had not come and made love to her there on his jacket in the grass of the orchard. But then she remembered how he had touched her and kissed her, and she felt the warmth flooding back through her. How would she hide from her mother, and the others assembled at the townhouse, the wonder and joy which she was still feeling?

She and her mother crossed the courtyard and passed through the gate to the street. Seeing them, the coachman opened the door and helped them up the step. Julia sat facing her mother. As before, she took the seat facing backwards.

The coach started moving over the cobblestones. "Now, tell me!" Julia said.

"Lady Cecilia arrived with the elderly earl, her maid, and a few footmen–"

Mrs. Brandon broke off and again looked closely at Julia. "You seem different, Julia." She reached out and smoothed Julia's hair, brushing something– probably leaves or blades of grass–from her hair. Julia looked down at her clothing. She retied the bow on her bodice and smoothed the lace.

"That garden grows wild!" Julia said, "The hedge was soft, and I almost fell asleep leaning back against it."

Her mother seemed to believe her. Why wouldn't she? How could she possibly guess the truth?

"So tell me what happened, Mama! Lady Cecilia arrived with the elderly earl, and then what?"

"After Lady Cecilia and the others arrived, in fine

141

carriages, of course, the hearing lasted less than ten minutes. Lady Cecilia told the magistrate that she had indeed written the letter, that Geoffrey had not abducted her or done anything at all against her will. The magistrate looked at the earl, and said, 'Your lordship, I trust you have no objection to setting this young man free.' The earl said, 'None at all.' The magistrate asked no other questions."

"What about the theft charge? Didn't someone also accuse him of stealing?"

"Yes, that's right. The magistrate asked about that. Geoffrey swore he was innocent. The magistrate said in the absence of evidence, Geoffrey was free to go."

"That was all? It was that easy?"

"With Lady Cecilia's word that she'd never been abducted, what else could the magistrate do except free Geoffrey?"

"What will Geoffrey do now? He'll have to earn a living."

"He is talking about applying to become an officer in his majesty's army.

Julia imagined her brother in a crisp red officer's uniform with brass buttons and gold braiding.

Her mother's voice softened when she said, "I saw the way they looked at each other, Lady Cecilia and Geoffrey. I think they are well-matched. Lady Cecilia is clearly a tempestuous and spirited girl."

"Oh, yes," said Julia, remembering the way she threw herself across the bed and wept, and the way she spoke her mind freely.

"Do you think they'll get married?" Mrs. Brandon asked.

"If her uncles don't find a way to stop her, and if she doesn't mind giving up her dowry."

Then, through the back window, Julia saw a rider following their coach. He stayed back far enough not to draw attention, but she knew from the shape of his shoulders that it was Lord Guildford following them.

The coach pulled to a stop in front of an imposing red brick, flat-fronted house of four or five stories. The windows were evenly spaced with intricate caps and moldings in the classical style. A crimson canopy was mounted over the front door.

The coachman opened the door. Julia and her mother stepped from the coach onto the pavement. Julia turned to see if Guildford was approaching, but he was nowhere in sight.

There was no need to knock at the townhouse door. As they approached, the door swung open. A butler greeted them and invited them in. "Mrs. Brandon and Miss Brandon, I presume?" he asked.

Julia's mother nodded her agreement.

The butler stood back while they entered, and announced their names. Just inside was a lushly furnished parlor. There were at least a dozen people in the room, which was spacious enough to hold everyone comfortably. Sofas and chairs were grouped around the room. A pianoforte stood in one corner.

As soon as Julia stepped inside, Lady Cecilia, who had been standing with Geoffrey, squealed and rushed toward her. Geoffrey stood watching, smiling.

Cecilia hugged her tightly and in her ear whispered, "It worked! It worked beautifully."

"I am so happy! But why was I summoned? What is going on?"

"I have no idea. Nobody does. The earl wanted

everyone together, all of us. Including you."

"I'd feel better about this whole thing," Julia whispered back, "if I hadn't crept from the house in the middle of the night with gold that didn't belong to me."

"I don't think anything bad is going to happen," Cecilia whispered. "The problem is, I have no idea what is going to happen."

Blanche waved to Cecilia from across the room. She was standing with Sam Mason. Something about the way they stood together made Julia know.

To Cecilia, she whispered, "Sam? And Blanche?"

"It looks that way," Cecilia whispered back. "They've asked for permission to leave service without notice."

"So Blanche will finally get her shop," said Julia. "I believe that brings two people to a perfect ending."

Geoffrey then came over and took her hands. Quietly he whispered, "Julia. My sweet and brave sister. Thank you."

"It's so good to see you, Geoffrey," she said, and it was. Prison hadn't dimmed his radiance or the brightness of his smile. There was no sign of injury to his arm. "Your arm has healed?"

"I'll carry a scar. He could have done far worse to me."

The door opened again, and Lord Guildford entered. The butler announced him. Julia didn't look at him. She was afraid to. She didn't think she could look at him without giving herself away. Geoffrey, seeing who entered, stood up straighter. To Julia, Geoffrey whispered, "That man knows how to handle a sword."

"So I understand," she responded.

Now she ventured a sidelong look at Guildford. He nodded slightly to acknowledge that he saw her, but to her vast relief, he had no intention of behaving familiarly toward her in front of this crowd and giving away how intimately he had touched her not long ago, in the garden inn. Once, when she was sixteen, she begged Geoffrey to tell her whether he was seeing in secret the daughter of one of their neighbors. Geoffrey said, "Never ask, Julia. A well-bred gentleman doesn't kiss and tell."

Blanche walked over to join them. "How odd, Julia. You and Lord Guildford are hardly looking at each other. I heard whisper among the footmen that he organized a search of London to find you. But he isn't even coming to talk to you now."

"I see you've gotten to know Sam Mason," Julia said.

"Don't change the subject, Julia," said Blanche. "Why is he acting as if he could care less that you're here? Did he find you this afternoon?"

Before Julia could respond, the door opened again and a half dozen people entered. Julia recognized Cecilia's uncles Jervis and Ashton and their wives. There were a few others, who she assumed were family members, who she had never seen before. Her chest constricted with apprehension. Had she known the uncles were coming, she might well have been too frightened to come.

"I wonder what your uncles are thinking now," Blanche whispered to Cecilia.

"I hope they're not thinking about how revenge this insult," said Cecilia. "My uncles have a great deal of power over me. Or rather, they have a great deal of power over my dowry. I hope they accept defeat gracefully, at least in the matter of Geoffrey's imprisonment."

Just then, a gentleman wearing a forest green waistcoat, matching breeches, and a white shirt with a sheer ruffle entered from the main part of the house through a set of double doors. Behind him came the elderly earl. When the earl entered, everyone quieted.

The gentleman wearing the green waistcoat cleared his throat to get everyone's attention, but calling for attention was unnecessary. Except for an occasional footstep or the rustling of a skirt, the room was now completely silent.

"My name is Richard Johnson," said the man in the green waistcoat. "Many of you already know me. I have served as the earl's personal solicitor for the past forty years. He has asked me to draw up some paperwork for him."

The earl seemed even weaker and more frail than before. The trip from Guildford Manor to London could not have been easy for him.

The earl and Mr. Johnson put their heads together and had a whispered conversation. Mr. Johnson led the earl to an elaborately carved and ornamented chair, with floral trails and openwork foliage, scrolling arms and a high arched back that made Julia think of a royal throne. The earl sat in the chair, still looking as frail and slight as ever, but the bulk and height of the chair made him seem larger.

Mr. Johnson said, "You have all been called here to be informed that the earl has decided to make two changes to his own will."

This was a surprise. Julia looked at her mother.

Why on earth had they been summoned for so personal a family matter? Then she stole a look at Lord Guildford, who was looking intently, and with puzzlement, from Mr. Johnson to the earl.

"As you all know," said Mr. Johnson, "because of his declining health, his lordship abdicated all rights and responsibilities belonging to his rank and position. He has no desire now to resume his authority, even if the law permitted him to renounce an abdication. As you may also know, the earl has retained authority over only two items of value, the deed to this townhouse, and the deed to Guildford Manor. His assumption always was, of course, that the deeds to these properties should pass to his great nephew, Robert Guildford, along with the title of earl and other property holdings."

Now Julia was afraid to look at Guildford, but for an entirely different reason. Was the earl taking away property which should, by right, be Guildford's to inherit? If so, why? The earl didn't strike her as the type to be angry, or punitive. Moreover, even if he was, why on earth would he want to punish Guildford?

"The first change," Mr. Johnson said, "is that his lordship plans to leave the deed to this townhouse to his niece, Lady Cecilia Guildford, for her to use as a dowry in the event she is unable to claim her own, so that she may marry whomever she pleases."

A ripple of amazement went through the room. Cecilia rushed to her great-uncle, and kissed his hand. Next she ran to Geoffrey and threw her arms around his neck. There, before the entire assembly, Geoffrey put his arms around her, too, and kissed her forehead. Julia looked at her mother, who was trying to hide her astonishment. Then she ventured a glance at Guildford, who was still watching the earl. He was stunned, but his brow was clear. Julia saw no anger in his countenance at all.

"However," Mr. Johnson continued, "the earl wishes to extract a promise from a certain Geoffrey Brandon. Mr. Brandon? Please step forward."

Geoffrey stepped forward. Mr. Johnson said, "His lordship understands that you have a tendency to wild behavior." He pointed a finger at Geoffrey and said, "He says you are to mend your wild ways. He trusts that the recent trouble you were in will be your last."

Geoffrey bowed both to Mr. Johnson and the earl. "Yes, your lordship. I have sworn to that already."

Mr. Johnson cleared his throat and said, "His lordship wishes to make one additional change. He will leave the deed to Guildford Manor to a lady who whose nobility of spirit has impressed him, a lady by the name of Julia Brandon."

Julia felt shock all through the room. For a moment, she was sure she had heard incorrectly. But everyone was staring at her. She felt as if she'd turned to stone.

"What?" Lord Guildford burst out. He stepped toward his uncle. "You are giving away my house?"

The earl actually smiled. He put his hands on the scrolled armrests of his chair and made a motion as if he wished to stand. Instantly both Mr. Johnson and Guildford hurried to assist him. Once he was on his feet, he looked directly at Guildford, and for the first time since he entered the room, he spoke. "No, Robert," he said, his voice shaky and quivery and weak, but perfectly understandable. "I am not giving away your house. I am giving away my house."

Someone nearby said, "He's gone mad."

The earl cleared his throat. "I heard that. I have not gone mad. I am setting matters right. Things are now as they should be." The strain of having spoken so many words at one time so taxed the old man's strength that his face seemed noticeably whiter. "Someone please help me back to my room."

Two family members sprang forward and took his arms and led him from the room.

Someone else said, "He can't do that!"

Suddenly it seemed everyone was talking at once–everyone except Julia, who stood without moving.

Mr. Johnson clapped for attention. To Lord Guildford, Mr. Johnson said, "The law is generally understood to require the full estate to pass to the legal heirs. You are free, of course, to question, or even challenge, the legality of the earl's new will."

"I would never do that!" Lord Guildford said, evidently pulling himself together after the shock.

Jervis Howard, who happened to be standing near Guildford, said, "It's nonsense, Robert." Lord Howard spoke softly, but the room was so silent–nobody moved at all–his voice carried to every corner. "That sort of will would never be upheld. He hasn't the authority to break up the holdings of an earldom."

"I have no desire to challenge the earl's wishes," said Guildford. "Besides, he may know what he's doing."

"What!" Lord Howard said. "Have you gone as crazy as him?"

All eyes were on Robert Guildford, and he was smiling. A man who takes delight in all life's

149

pleasures would also, naturally, take delight when events turn absurd. "Besides," he said with an exaggerated flourish of his arm to show he was speaking to the entire assembly, "I happen to know an easy way to get my house back."

He looked for Julia. Finding her, he walked toward her, still smiling. Everyone stood back, watching them.

Since leaving the inn, Julia had not been able to look him full in the face because she knew what would happen: she would remember how he had touched her in the shadows of the inn's orchard, and she would blush.

This was exactly what happened, with everyone watching. She looked into his face as he approached her, and the memory came back to her, setting her all aquiver and weakening her limbs. She knew from the warmth that spread over her face and chest that she was flushing.

Guildford took Julia's hand and said, as much to everyone present as to Julia, "The easier way to get my house back, is to convince Julia Brandon to marry me."

When hubbub erupted in the room, with everyone it seemed talking at once, he held her open palm to his heart. He was smiling, the joy back in his face.

He whispered, "This, I think, is love."

Epilogue

Julia and Robert were married within the week. Mrs. Brandon encouraged the ceremony to be held as soon as possible, not because, as someone cynical might suppose, she was eager for Julia to make such a splendid marriage and assure herself the title of Lady Guildford, but because she'd seen the looks that passed between Julia and Lord Guildford and she was terrified that if the wedding were not held quickly, her daughter and Lord Guildford would end up bedded together before the ceremony could take place. It simply didn't occur to her, knowing her well-behaved and chaste daughter, that such already occurred, and in fact, continued to occur in secret during the week before the ceremony.

The wedding was held in the chapel of Guildford Manor. Afterward Julia remembered very little about the ceremony–other than that she managed to say "I do" at the correct time. The ring Guildford slipped on her finger was the beautiful sapphire that had belonged to his mother. "I always meant for you to have it," he whispered.

Geoffrey and Cecilia sat in the first pew, holding hands. Their own wedding would be celebrated the following Saturday, and afterward, they would live in the Guildford Townhouse. Geoffrey was wearing his new officer's uniform. Mr. Brandon, whose back was recovering, and who sat with his wife in the chapel, had said–upon seeing his son in uniform–"Good. If you get into another fight, I trust it will be on behalf of his majesty and not your runaway passions."

For Julia, the wedding supper, like the ceremony itself, passed by as if it were a dream. Ladies and gentlemen, Guildford family members, dressed as sumptuously as if they were being presented to the king, congratulated her and told her she looked beautiful. Ladies admired her dress, which she'd had hurriedly made for the occasion, made of white satin trimmed with blue and gold.

After the wedding supper, the musicians played. Guildford took Julia's arm and asked her to dance.

She walked with him to the dance floor to lead the minuet, remembering the last time he'd wanted to dance with her. Who could have guessed that when she finally danced with him, it would be at their wedding?

The next day, she and Guildford moved into the largest set of rooms in Guildford Manor. After Cecilia and Geoffrey were married and living in the London Townhouse, Julia and Cecilia were frequent visitors in each other's homes. They enjoyed London life, visiting the shopping districts during the day, and the theatre districts in the evenings with their husbands– and they always bought their gloves in the glove shop on Oxford Street owned by Blanche and Sam.

ABOUT ANNE KINSEY

To learn more about Anne and her forthcoming fiction, please visit Anne's website at http://www.AnneKinsey.com. If you have any comments or questions, she would love to hear from you.